I0655733

Witchin

THE COMPLETE SERIES

CHARITY PARKERSON

—Warning: This book is intended for readers over the age of 18.

 Created with Vellum

Introduction

Witchin Warlock: Caspian comes from a long line of witches. Brock is third generation F.B.I. They shouldn't fit but they do.*Witchin Solstice*: Special Agent Brock Wray is on the case of another weird crime. Strange enough to need the help of his warlock husband. This time, they can't do it alone.*Witchin Moonbeam*: There's another mystery in Elvenwood. This time, the police are on the case. It's not going well.*Witchin Wildcat*: In the small town of Elvenwood, everyone knows everyone else. That makes it hard to meet new people. It's a good thing they're being overrun by a new population: supernatural creatures.*Witchin Fangs*: With the town's supernatural community trying to shore up the magic wall around their borders, they're getting overwhelmed. They need someone who moves fast and is awake all night. Caspian knows just the guy.*Witchin Yuletide*: Elevenwood has a new citizen, and he has a big... personality. Thankfully, there's a vet in town who can handle him.

Introduction for Witchin Warlock

Caspian comes from a long line of witches. Brock is third generation F.B.I. They shouldn't fit, but they do.

A year ago, Caspian moved to a small town in Ohio. He hoped the lack of competition in the area would be good for his psychic business, Futures Untold. The last thing he expected was a sexy F.B.I. agent to show up and treat him like a missing person's bloodhound. Even though Caspian keeps doing favors for Special Agent Brock Wray, his distrust of authority runs deep. After all, they used to drown witches in this area back in the day, and Caspian has no desire to end up on Brock's missing persons' list.

Officially, no one knows how Brock keeps solving so many huge cases. Caspian is Brock's secret weapon. The man knows things no one should. That's not why Brock keeps showing up and making excuses to see Caspian. Caspian fascinates Brock. Not only does Brock's inner detective need to know how Caspian knows so much, but Caspian is also smoking hot. He is the single most gorgeous man to step foot in their tiny town in ages. Brock isn't dumb. He has to take Caspian off the market as quickly as possible and he'll use any excuse to get close enough to do it.

When Brock takes Caspian along for the ride on a case, things will get weird. Let's hope Caspian isn't forced to show why he's the most witchin warlock around or Brock might run for the hills.

Witchin Warlock *is a fun short story just in time for Halloween.*

Chapter One

EVERY GOOD WITCH, wizard, warlock, psychic, medium, or whatever a person chose to identify as knew New Orleans was the place to be to showcase the best powers. However, there were a few issues with that way of thinking. For one, New Orleans was hot. It smelled funny, and every witch, wizard, warlock, psychic, and medium knew it was the place to be to freely showcase their magic. That meant competition out the wazoo. So, when Caspian's great aunt—the one and only Magical Margo—died and left Caspian her Tarot and Medium shoppe, Caspian immediately sold out and headed north.

Even real spell casters needed a shtick if they hoped to drum up clientele. Margo had talked to ghosts.

People had come from far and wide to talk to their children, parents, and spouses on the other side. Margo hadn't been a real medium. She had been a real witch, and she had taught Caspian that with the right spell, anything was possible. Unfortunately, Caspian didn't have what it took to comfort grieving family members. What Caspian could do was predict the future with flair, and—unfortunately—he could also catch the eye of the Ohio branch office of the F.B.I.

That was why Special Agent Brock Wray currently stared a hole in the side of Caspian's head while Caspian finished with his client, Clara. Clara came to him each week. All she really wanted was a friend to chat with. Despite that, she had paid to be there. Brock had not, so Brock could just wait with his fancy hair and too tight suit. Goddamn. It was getting kind of hot inside his shop.

"I know you said my soulmate has dark brown hair, but Chad has blond hair, and I really think he's the one."

"No one named Chad is ever the one," Caspian said, barely hanging on to his temper, with Brock still staring at him.

Brock chuckled and then tried covering the sound with a cough.

Caspian had been in Elvenwood, Ohio for almost a year and had a good clientele. He loved Clara dearly. She paid him good money for these weekly chats, but she was also dumb as a box of rocks. He could tell her the first and last name of her soulmate. Hell, with the right spell work, Caspian could give her the guy's social security number. What he couldn't do was make her quit falling for every loser along the way.

Clara's brown eyes narrowed. She rubbed her chin. "You know, I have thought it was a little weird that Chad doesn't answer his phone past a certain time each night. He says his wife left him last year, and he has his small kids, so he doesn't want the phone waking them, but it's weird. Like all he has to do is turn off his ringer and check it occasionally. It's not fucking rocket science. There's no need to disappear from the planet all because the kids are asleep."

Brock sat forward, as if really getting into the conversation. "You're not talking about Chad Bowman, are you?"

Clara twisted in her seat. "Yeah. Do you know him?"

Brock nodded. "I picked him up on Grindr six months ago. His wife didn't leave him. She's pregnant with his fourth kid. He tried to pull that same shit on me, but I investigate everyone I date."

"Are you fucking kidding me? That rat bastard."

That was the thing about a small town. It was hard to get away with anything. Too many people knew each other.

Clara looked Caspian's way. Her shoulders fell. "I guess you're right. It's not him."

Caspian nodded. "Dark hair. Look out for dark hair. He also has blue eyes, if that helps. I sense you've already met, but you've been too preoccupied to notice. Make sure you open your mind. You'll find him. He's already noticed you."

Clara brightened. "Really? Well, I guess I'd better go. I have to dump Chad before my shift starts at the store. Next week, same time?"

"I've got you on my calendar," Caspian assured her as he stood and walked her to the door. They hugged and said their final goodbyes before Caspian turned his attention Brock's way. "So you picked up Chad on Grindr? Special Agent Wray, I never would have guessed."

Brock's dark blue eyes flashed with humor. "In my defense, who hasn't thought someone named Chad was the one?"

"Fair," Caspian said, clearing away his tarot cards. They were useless to him. He only used them for show. Every snippet Caspian saw of the future came from a potion he drank before each appointment. "What brings you my way, agent?"

Brock's mouth lifted in one corner in a sexy smirk. Caspian hated that he noticed. His entire life, Margo had drilled into his head a mistrust of authorities. He had a gift. Normal people would use him for it. People like Brock would have him committed. After all, it was the authorities that used to drown witches in these parts.

"You don't like me, do you?" Brock said, as if reading Caspian's mind.

Caspian pasted on a bright smile, refusing to admit any such thing. "What an odd thing to say. You didn't answer my question."

Brock shook his head and sighed. "We have a missing person. A local bus driver didn't show up for his route. Sheriff Kennedy went to his house. The door was open, but there didn't seem to be anything missing. There was no sign of the guy. His bus and personal vehicle were still in the driveway. His wallet was on the dresser and his shoes were by the door. It's like he simply vanished. After a search of the local area, Lonnie called me."

A smile snapped to Caspian's lips without his permission. "It must be a slow day at the F.B.I. if I was the first person you thought to visit."

Brock held his stare. Caspian's skin tingled with awareness of the other man's large presence in his tiny shop. "I'm not here on behalf of the bureau. I'm just a concerned citizen today, looking for a neighbor."

Caspian's eyebrows rose. "And you came to me? I don't know any bus drivers."

"You know things, Caspian. Don't pretend you don't. You've helped out law enforcement in the past. No one knows the things you do. Hell, I'm willing to bet money you know the name of Clara's soulmate, but you're not saying so you can milk her for every dime."

"A man has to eat," Caspian shot back, unashamed.

A slow smile spread across Brock's lips, making it a little harder for Caspian to breathe. He really fucking hated that he found Brock so hot. "Who is it?"

"Scott." Damn it. He could kick himself. It was like Brock had some magical hold on Caspian's dumb brain.

A bark of laughter burst from Brock. "The manager at the grocery store?"

Caspian nodded. "He's her boss, so he doesn't want to make a move, and she's too busy with the Chads of the world to notice he's sickeningly in love with her."

Brock's bright smile slipped away. "Help me, Caspian. I won't tell anyone how you do it."

A sigh gathered in Caspian's throat. Caspian swallowed it down. He was such a sucker for blue eyes and nice shoulders. "Fine. I need something of his." His spell was wearing off from his visit with Clara.

He hadn't expected to do two readings today without a recharge.

Brock visibly tried hiding his triumph as he passed a set of keys with a fake rabbit's foot attached Caspian's way.

Caspian's fingers wrapped around the keys. He took a breath and closed his eyes. Immediately, the vision of a yellow school bus speeding past waiting children filled Caspian's head. Then it was gone. He didn't get more. The effects of his earlier potion were gone. Still, that was odd.

Caspian tilted his head to one side and considered what he had seen. "I thought you said his bus was still in the driveway."

"It is. Why?"

"Huh." Caspian shook his head. "I need more time. My visions aren't making sense. I'll need to commune with the dead." He wanted Brock to think he was strange. Caspian didn't know why. He just enjoyed seeing how much bullshit Brock would swallow to get his next lead.

To Caspian's surprise, Brock smiled. "Fine. Keep the keys. I'll pick you up around... seven?"

Caspian blinked. "For what?"

"Our date," Brock said, as if they had discussed the matter a dozen times. "The fall festival starts at five, but I'd rather let things die down a bit. I don't want to fight a crowd of kids."

"Um..."

"See you at seven," Brock said as he headed for the door.

Caspian stared at the front door of his shop for five minutes after Brock left. His mind grappled with the idea of dating an F.B.I. agent. No good could come of that. That ass, though. Brock's did look firm. What the fuck was he supposed to do now?

A SMILE PULLED at the corners of Brock's mouth, making his cheeks ache as he left Caspian's shop, Futures Untold. He loved the disgruntled way Caspian always tolerated his presence. It always put a little extra pep in his step, keeping Caspian off guard. All the gay men for three towns around had their sights set on the brown-eyed beauty. Caspian had the body of a Greek god and a smile so wicked, he nearly made Brock pant the first time they met. Brock couldn't explain why he enjoyed Caspian's irritation so much, but he always felt closer to winning him when Caspian growled at him. He knew he shouldn't claim they had a date until he actually had Caspian outside his shop, but they had a date. He couldn't wait. Elvenwood's annual Halloween Fall Festival was the best around, and this was Brock's favorite season. He loved everything about Halloween. The air had a certain scent. He wasn't a fan of kids, but he remembered the excitement of dressing up and getting candy from strangers. Brock loved staying up, eating junk, and watching scary movies. There was an excitement in the air. He should probably feel a little guilty for using Frank Steeler's disappearance as a reason to see Caspian, but that was part and parcel with his profession. Everything was doom and gloom. At least, this way, some good came from the everyday wretchedness. He was dying to know what happened to Frank, though. The guy had lived in this town his whole life. He had been a bus driver for forty years without missing a day. It made no sense for him to vanish without a trace.

"Hey there, Agent Wray. Can we expect to see you tonight at the festival?"

Brock slid into his usual booth at Clark's diner. "I'll be there."

His waitress, Debbie, had been asking him the same question every day at lunch for a week. His answer never changed. He knew she hoped for more, but he never gave in. Brock very decidedly swung the other way.

"Would you like your regular?"

He flashed the buxom blonde a smile. "Please and thank you." He knew he was a little boring and could probably save money by packing the same thing for lunch every day rather than ordering it, but he liked the atmosphere at Clark's. Not to mention, Brock lived alone and spent a good eighty percent of his time by himself. It was nice to have some interaction with other people.

Debbie brought him his usual tea and veggie sandwich. "I heard Mr. Steeler has gone missing. Do you have any leads?"

Even though Brock technically shouldn't talk about any cases outside the office, in this case, there was nothing to tell. "Not yet."

"I'm surprised you didn't learn anything from Caspian. That boy, if I didn't know better, I'd swear he really is psychic."

First off, this town never ceased to amaze him. He had just left Caspian's shop, and everyone already knew where he had been. Second, it was hilarious to him to hear Debbie call Caspian a boy when they were likely the same age. Last, she wasn't wrong. More than once, Brock had mused over Caspian's abilities. They were uncanny. But at the end of the day, Brock didn't really believe in all that nonsense.

"He's definitely highly intuitive. In this case, though, I think it'll take him some time to wade through the intricacies of the case."

Debbie nodded. Her ponytail bobbed along with her head. She didn't leave him alone to eat. His discomfort grew. "Speaking of tonight's festival..."

Fuck.

"I was thinking..."

Goddamn it.

The bell above the door jingled as it was shoved open harder than necessary. All heads turned that way. An aggravated-looking Caspian glanced over his shoulder at the bell like it was to blame for his over-the-top entrance. Brock hid a smile. He found everything about Caspian adorable.

Caspian scanned the diner. His gaze landed on Brock, and he barreled Brock's way. Debbie took a step back as Caspian plopped down across from Brock and slapped Frank's keys down on the table. "He's dead."

Debbie gasped.

Caspian tossed her a quick glance. "Oh. Hey, Deb. Could I get a Coke?"

"Of course." She raced away, obviously way more excited to tell her bit of gossip more than she was about grabbing Caspian a drink.

Brock didn't bother retrieving the keys. "That didn't take long."

Caspian shrugged and stole a chip from Brock's plate. "When you handed me the keys earlier, I saw a yellow bus speeding past groups of kids waiting at their stops. That struck me as odd since you said he didn't show up for work and his bus was in the drive-way. When you left, I drank some tonic."

"Tonic?"

Caspian shook his head. "Coffee."

"You said tonic."

"Well, I meant coffee," Caspian said, sounding irri-tated over Brock's interruptions. "Anyhow, I drank some coffee, and everything cleared in my head. When he got on the bus this morning, there was someone waiting inside, and they ambushed him. After they... did the deed, they drove him out to the old, abandoned sawmill, dumped his body, and then drove the bus back to his place."

Damn, that was... detailed. "Where were you around that time this morning?"

Caspian didn't as much as flinch, even though he had to know it was suspicious for him to know that much detail. "Jogging, as always. I ran into Susan Tolbert and spent thirty minutes listening to her bitch about her cheating husband. I'm sure she'd be glad to vouch for as much."

Brock's shoulders relaxed. "Yeah. Geoff's been cheating with Naomi down at the store for a few months now. To be fair, though, Susan has been sleeping with Naomi down at the store for months now too. I'm glad you have an alibi and I hope you understand why I had to ask."

Caspian shrugged and stole another chip. "I know too much. I get it. It's been like this my whole life." He popped the chip in his mouth and chewed while staring off into the distance. When he met Brock's stare again, Brock fought a sigh. He was truly beautiful, even though he looked sad. "For the record, if you plan to accuse me of something every time you ask for my help, I'd rather you not ask again. In small town terms, I haven't lived here all that long. If people start to think there's something wrong with me, my business will suffer. I don't want to have to move."

Guilt hit harder than Brock expected. In his line of work, he saw all the bad in people. This one time, he didn't want to be that guy. It wasn't fair for him to ask for Caspian's help and then crucify him for it. Brock definitely didn't want Caspian's business to suffer or for Caspian to move. He pushed his plate to the center of the table so Caspian could share. "Sorry about that. I always appreciate your help and I wouldn't come to you if thought there was anything wrong with you. In fact, I like you a lot."

Debbie appeared with Caspian's Coke. "Can I get you anything else?"

Caspian didn't look away from Brock. "No, thank you."

Debbie left them alone, and they continued staring at each other.

"So, you really have visions, huh?"

Caspian nodded. "Yep."

"Who's your soulmate, then?"

Caspian didn't smile as Brock hoped. He shrugged. "I never look at my future."

"You should."

"Why? Do you think it's you?"

Brock nodded. "Yep."

They went back to staring at each other in silence.

Brock nudged his plate even closer. "Do you want half of my sandwich?"

"I'm a vegetarian."

"It's a veggie sandwich."

"I don't think I can eat after the things I saw."

They dropped their gazes to Brock's plate. Half his chips were gone. Brock didn't call Caspian on it, and Caspian didn't look guilty. They went back to staring at each other.

"I guess we should go find this body."

"Better bring a shovel."

Brock winced. "That bad, huh?"

Caspian nodded.

"Well." Brock dug out his wallet and dropped a twenty on the table. "I still say we should get to it.

The quicker we get back, the faster I can get to fucking you."

"Okay."

Damn. Brock had never been more excited to dig up a body in his life.

Chapter Two

THEY MADE the drive into the middle of nowhere in mostly silence. Occasionally, Caspian broke it by giving details of his vision when he recognized a landmark. Otherwise, Caspian didn't know what to say. Brock thought they were soulmates and he planned to fuck Caspian later. It had been a strange day.

When they came to the area where they would have to walk the rest of the way, they climbed from the car, donned their jackets, and Brock grabbed a shovel. They headed through the trees. It was an oddly pleasant walk, considering they were on their way to find a dead person.

Caspian couldn't stop tossing glances Brock's way. He genuinely was a gorgeous guy. Caspian had always tried avoiding those thoughts, since Brock could ruin him. Brock had seemed to believe that Caspian had powers. Caspian didn't know where to go with that. Margo had always said Caspian would know when he had met the one. He would recognize him by the man's acceptance. Now Caspian was off his game, thanks to musing over it.

Brock suddenly threw out his arm, stopping Caspian from taking another step, and pulling Caspian's mind back on track. There was an open man-sized hole in the ground. It was empty. Caspian went on high alert. Something wasn't right. Frank should be in that hole. The slightest rustling sound behind them was all the warning they got before Brock was knocked to the ground. Frank came at him, teeth gnashing. Without thinking, ancient words sprang to Caspian's lips and a blue light shot from Caspian's hands, sending Frank flying. A goddamn zombie. Caspian hadn't seen one in years. He should have known, since the moon phase was right and it was the start of the day of the dead... literally.

Brock scrambled back to his feet. "What the fuck?"

Frank leapt through the air, coming for Brock again. Caspian tackled Brock to the ground, covering his body. He ended up molded against Brock, their faces only inches apart. "Stay down. I've got this," Caspian promised. Before he could stop himself, he pressed a quick kiss to Brock's lips and rolled away. He kept his body between Brock and Frank, physically blocking Frank's advance. Frank had no interest in Caspian. Caspian didn't smell like a human. He smelled like magic, which didn't appeal to most flesh-eating beasts.

Frank shuffled closer, visibly looking for his opening to get to the only thing he cared about: food. His dead eyes and pale face didn't unnerve Caspian anywhere near as much as the massive amount of flesh missing from Frank's neck. It was obvious he had been feasted upon before being left to turn. Caspian searched for some way to protect Brock without using his magic. There was a tiny chance Brock had missed his use of his magic while face down on the ground earlier. Now he had Brock's full attention. He couldn't hide.

His gaze landed on the shovel Brock had dropped when he had been attacked. Before he could lunge for the weapon, he was shoved aside. Frank sprang forward and shots rang out. The bullets slowed Frank long enough for Caspian to grab the shovel. Frank collided with Brock, taking him to the ground again. Caspian swung. The sharp edge of the shovel collided with bone and dislodged Frank's barely hanging on head. Brock shoved his way out from beneath what was left of Frank's body. His every breath came out sounding like he had just finished a marathon. He was wild-eyed and looked ready to faint.

"What the fuck?" he said between heavy breaths. "I mean, what the actual fuck?"

Caspian shook his head. "I don't know, dude. Swamp gas?"

Brock's crazed gaze swung Caspian's way. "Swamp gas? Have you lost your goddamn mind? Why are you so calm? You just took off a guy's head with a shovel. He tried to fucking eat me."

Caspian shrugged. "He was going to hurt you. It seemed a pretty easy decision from there."

Brock dragged his fingers through his hair, making a mess of his normally perfectly styled mane. "I have to call this in. We have to preserve the scene." He was obviously on the verge of completely freaking out and Caspian couldn't risk any more exposure. Caspian dropped the shovel. He closed the space between them and claimed Brock's lips. As their tongues stroked, Caspian almost forgot to take control of Brock's mind. He hadn't expected such an amazing kiss. Damn. They were pursuing this. Later. Right now, Caspian had business.

He took a step back, leaving Brock frozen. Even though his body was on fire, he got to work. While chanting ancient spells, Caspian used the power of his blood and ancestors to move Frank's body and head back into the ground. The dirt slid into the hole, covering the body. Once the ground reclaimed the hole, grass and flowers grew, making the new grave invisible. Next, he swiped away the stains from their clothes and the shovel. Once all signs of their struggle and Frank were gone, Caspian stepped back inside Brock's hold and reclaimed his mouth.

Their tongues brushed. Brock's fingers found Caspian's hair. Caspian moaned when Brock tightened his hold on Caspian's messy locks. He almost forgot this had been a means to an end. He wanted Brock. There was no denying it.

Brock pulled away, but he didn't release Caspian. He stared at Caspian through a hooded gaze, setting Caspian's body ablaze even more than their kiss had. "Right now, we have to find that sawmill, but later..." Brock held his stare. "... later, you're mine."

Caspian's breath left his lungs. He had wanted no one more, and he hated himself for it. Brock carried a badge. No good could come of them being together. Caspian already knew he wouldn't stop, though. He wanted Brock. Nothing would stop him from having him. Something had already begun between them. There was no going back now.

Brock's body burned as they made their way through the woods toward the old, abandoned sawmill. It had been a nice day. He had no idea what had driven him to ambush Caspian with that kiss, but he regretted nothing. The sawmill came into view, and Brock went on alert. He became hyper-aware he was the only protection between Caspian and a possible murderer. Brock didn't know what he had been thinking, bringing Caspian along. Caspian had told him the body had been dumped at the sawmill. He should have brought another agent with him. He had to keep Caspian safe.

Brock quietly moved a few steps ahead of Caspian and pulled out his service weapon. There were too many windows and open doorways. They could be walking into anything. Caspian seemed oddly relaxed, as if he marched into danger every day.

"There's so much rotting wood and piles of debris. You might need to come out here with dogs or ground-penetrating equipment. I doubt we'll find anything."

Caspian's claim had Brock's shoulders relaxing. It gave him the excuse he needed to get Caspian out of there before he got hurt. Caspian just knew so damn much that he seemed more capable than most. That was all the excuse Brock could muster for why he had put Caspian in danger to begin with. He would be more careful in the future. There was a bad feeling in his gut about this case. Brock had to get Caspian out of there.

"You're right. We should head back to the car."

They turned to head back the way they came. The sound of tinkling glass—like a window had shattered in the distance— sent Brock spinning back toward the building. He eyed the windows, trying to decide where the sound had come from. A quick movement by a downstairs window caught his attention. Brock focused on the spot. The outline of a head peeked out before darting out of sight again.

Brock shoved Caspian behind him. "Wait here."

Caspian didn't listen. He latched on to Brock's back and walked in step with him.

Brock cast an annoyed look over his shoulder. "I said stay put."

"No," Caspian whispered, as if people were listening. "If you're putting your life in danger by not calling for backup, I'll have to be your backup."

Brock rolled his eyes. "How is protecting you going to help me? You're not even armed."

"I'm armed with charms. I've got you."

Despite the seriousness of the situation, a snort escaped Brock. He liked Caspian a lot more than he had liked anyone in a long time. He definitely hadn't dated anyone willing to put themselves in danger to guard his back. Every second they spent together; the more Brock wanted.

True to his word, Caspian stuck to Brock's back as Brock cleared the door of the sawmill. Their footsteps sounded loud in the otherwise silent building. In the years since the sawmill shut down, dust, debris, and animals had claimed the building. Sunlight streamed through the broken windows. Dust hung in the air, visible to the naked eye in the rays of light cutting through the room. Rats didn't bother hiding. Brock and Caspian were the intruders.

As they rounded the corner into the room where Brock had seen the mystery face in the window, an unnatural-sounding growl rent the air. Birds and other small wildlife scattered. A man who looked ragged and homeless charged Brock. At the last second, Brock caught sight of the ax he held and fired. His shot hit its mark, striking the man between the eyes. For a moment, he froze. Caspian whispered something Brock couldn't hear through the ringing in his ears from the gunfire. The guy dropped. His ax flew into the air, landing perfectly to sever the man's head. Brock turned away from the sight. He sucked air, pulling years of dust into his lungs. As he fell into a coughing fit, Caspian rubbed his back.

"Now might be a good time to call this in."

He was so calm and steady. The bureau needed to hire Caspian. He had what it took.

Brock nodded. He dug his keys out and passed them Caspian's way. "Take my car and head back to town. I'll catch a ride back when all this is cleared up. You shouldn't be stuck out here the rest of the day."

Caspian cast a look around, as if assessing if it was safe to leave Brock before nodding. "All right. If you're sure I shouldn't stay."

His stomach still churned, and Brock didn't want to puke in front of Caspian. He swiped at his mouth, hoping he could hold back. "Yeah. You have nothing to do with this and I'm sure you have other things to do with your time. I'll see you tonight."

With another nod, Caspian accepted his keys. "Okay. Be careful." He kissed Brock's cheek.

Brock watched him go with his heart in his throat. One day soon, they would have to talk about them. It wouldn't happen with a headless body only feet away. It was best if Brock focused on the case in front of him. Tonight, though, he would have his moment with Caspian. It was time they made things real.

Chapter Three

CASPIAN SPENT his afternoon pacing the floor. He had gotten lucky with his last-second spell to behead that zombie. It looked to be a fairly recent turn, so—likely—in autopsy, he would just look like a crazy cannibal. Caspian couldn't keep taking risks. He had to live in this town. Caspian didn't want to end up back in New Orleans because he couldn't be himself anywhere else. He liked this weird little town filled with cheating spouses and hopeless romantics. Caspian stopped pacing. He liked Brock. It was time he stopped pretending he didn't. Caspian didn't know where to go with that. Margo would likely turn over in her grave.

A knock landed on the door, pulling Caspian from his musings. Caspian answered. Brock stood on the other side. His jacket was gone, and his sleeves were rolled up to his elbows. He looked tired. For a moment, they simply stared at each other.

"Hi."

A smile pulled at the corners of Caspian's mouth. "Hi."

Brock shuffled from foot to foot, looking adorably nervous. "So, are you ready to bob for apples and eat kettle corn?"

"Not really." But he would if that was what it took to spend more time with Brock.

"Thank god. One headless guy a day is enough for me," Brock said, stepping over the threshold and shocking Caspian.

Caspian's house was warded against intrusion. No one could come inside without invitation, which meant one thing. This house was meant to be Brock's house too. Caspian didn't have time to reel with that discovery. Brock kicked the door closed behind him and overcame Caspian. Their mouths met, and they immediately tore at each other's clothes. All the times Caspian had growled and scowled at Brock rose to the surface, revealing Caspian's irritation for what it was: unwanted lust. He wasn't supposed to feel this way about any authority figure. Caspian didn't want to fall for someone he would have to keep his magic hidden from for the rest of his life. That's why his kind almost always stuck with their own. He had too many potions and natural abilities he would have to keep secret. Caspian didn't want to want this. His body and heart didn't care about any amount of logic. He was on fire.

"Where's your bedroom?" Brock asked between kisses.

Caspian took Brock's hand and led him toward the bedroom. Brock didn't make small talk. He simply towed Caspian into his arms and took him down onto the bed the moment they were close enough to do so. Brock's hands were everywhere. Despite his best efforts not to use his magic, Caspian used a little umph to help undress Brock a bit faster.

Brock kissed his way down Caspian's body. "Where do you keep your condoms?"

Caspian's mind froze. "Um. I don't have any."

Brock's head lifted. Their gazes met. "You don't?"

Caspian shook his head. Not only was he impervious to diseases, but Caspian also didn't sleep around. "No." He tried to explain. Even to his ears, he sounded uncomfortable. "Yeah, I don't... I mean, there's no one."

Brock nodded, as if he understood. He rolled away. Disappointment washed over Caspian. It was hard being different from everyone else. He liked not having competition here, but it was lonely being the only warlock for hundreds of miles.

Brock picked his jeans up off the floor. Defeat weighed heavily on Caspian's chest. Brock found his wallet and dug out a condom and a tiny sample-sized lube. A bright smile lit Brock's face. "Thank god. It's been so long; I couldn't remember if I had anything in my wallet."

Relief took Caspian's breath. Brock wasn't leaving. He crawled between Caspian's thighs and stared down at Caspian. "You're gorgeous. I could stare at you all day."

Caspian fought an unexpected blush. "Thank you. The feeling is mutual." He really could. Brock was one of those guys who was always perfectly put together. His hair was always styled, and his clothes always matched. He had a polish Caspian could never achieve. Caspian always wanted to touch him. He smelled nice too.

Brock slowly lowered his head.

Caspian watched him until the very last second. His eyes didn't close until their lips met. The muscles in his stomach clenched. His heart swelled with emotion. He didn't want this to be a one-night stand. Brock ran his hand down Caspian's torso, shaping every inch of Caspian, as if he had wanted to do so for a long time. A sharp pain took Caspian's breath when Brock nipped at his bottom lip. Then, in a flash, Caspian found himself on his stomach and clinging to the headboard while Brock kissed and bit a path down his body. He heard plastic crinkle as teeth sank into his ass cheek. Caspian's spine bowed. His skin burned.

Brock dragged Caspian's hips back and up until Caspian was on his knees. Wet fingers probed his asshole, stretching him. Moans vibrated in Caspian's throat. Then the blunt, wide head of Brock's cock pressed against the tight ring of muscles surrounding Caspian's asshole. Caspian fought the urge to beg. Brock thrust. A cry tore from Caspian's lips at the sudden intrusion.

"Fuck. I'm sorry. Damn. You feel good." Brock held still, giving Caspian time to adjust. "I'm sorry," he said again, but his hips rolled, belying his words.

Caspian clung to the headboard as Brock thrust again. He hit right where Caspian wanted him. A moan escaped him. Caspian squeezed his eyes closed and fought the magic inside him that wanted to rise to the surface. Cries that were out of his control reverberated from the walls as Brock slammed inside him over and over again. His dick leaked onto the mattress. Caspian's skin felt too tight. Pressure built, drawing his balls up as the spring inside him wound tighter. Caspian bit into his pillow. Electricity popped and crackled around his hands. He knew without looking there would a slight blue glow emanating from his palms. To give his powers an outlet, Caspian muttered an ancient spell beneath his breath, adding to the pleasure of their coupling.

Brock made a strangled sound.

Ecstasy tore through Caspian. Cum shot from his cock, soaking the blankets beneath him. Caspian openly humped the air, taking what he wanted from Brock's dick.

Brock's thrusts turned almost violent as he came. Indecipherable words came out in gasps from Brock's lips. His fingers dug into Caspian's skin with enough force to leave bruises. All Caspian knew was euphoria. Wave after wave of tiny deaths took him. He gasped his way through the multiple orgasms his spell created. Later, he would pat himself on the back for the earthquake-worthy orgasm he knew Brock experienced. Brock would never have another orgasm without thinking of him. Right now, Caspian couldn't think at all. The moment owned him. They collapsed into a heap of sweaty limbs. Brock placed light kisses on Caspian's ear—like he couldn't stop silently praising him.

"Wow. Goddamn. That was. You are. Goddamn. I'm shook."

A chuckle escaped Caspian. He couldn't stop it from happening. In all his years, he had never been happier than he was in that moment with a rambling

Brock sweating all over him. He never wanted the night to end.

———

WITH DARKNESS SURROUNDING THEM, Brock held Caspian. He couldn't stop petting and kissing him. Never in all his thirty-six years had he experienced anything like sex with Caspian. His orgasm had been so intense, he swore he came several times and lost sight in one eye for a minute. In one encounter, Brock knew it was over for him. Well, honestly, before they had sex, Brock had already known he had met the one. But after sex, Caspian might have to physically toss him out if he wanted to rid himself of Brock. In his mind, Brock had already moved in, and they were six months into a forever marriage. This was the one for him. There was no going back.

"How did things go after I left?"

Brock stroked Caspian's stomach and kissed the shell of his ear one more time because he couldn't stop. "Uneventful. We didn't find Frank, but we found his blood and other chunks of him around the mill. There's little doubt he's dead, as you said. It looks like he just had an unfortunate encounter with a crazy transient. I don't think anyone else is in danger."

Caspian nodded. He turned his head and kissed Brock, making Brock's heart swell. "You were brave today. Thank you for keeping me safe."

Damn. Brock didn't think Caspian had needed him at all, but he loved hearing the praise. Caspian was intoxicating and addicting. Brock never wanted to be anywhere else. "I would never let anything happen to you." That much was absolutely true. Whether or not Caspian recognized it, he belonged to Brock. Brock would give his life to keep Caspian safe. "I have a question, though."

Caspian hummed against Brock's lips, trying to kiss him into silence.

This was too important for Brock to let Caspian distract him. He held Caspian's jaw, forcing Caspian to meet his stare. Caspian looked slightly nervous. Brock couldn't have that. They had danced around each other for too long now. "Would you be mine? Like officially? I mean, like I only date you and you only date me, and if people ask, I get to say you're my boyfriend."

A smile exploded across Caspian's face. "Yeah. I'd like that."

Happiness had Brock springing into action. He lunged, covering Caspian's body with his and capturing his mouth. Their tongues met and brushed. Their hard cocks strained to get closer like they hadn't already blown once tonight. Brock couldn't wait to get started on this forever thing. They were one thousand percent meant to be. He had never been happier.

Chapter Four

CASPIAN'S HEAD was completely in the clouds. He knew he should pay closer attention to his client, but it was hard, so hard with Brock nearby. His tiny shop seemed hotter and smaller than usual. Caspian fought the urge to scream for Clara to leave so he could properly fuck the man who owned one hundred percent of Caspian's thoughts.

"So I started seeing someone from work."

Caspian hummed. He already knew, since he'd drunk his potion already today, Clara still wasn't seeing the right person from work.

"I really think she's the one."

"She's not the one."

Clara's shoulders fell at Caspian's claim. "Really? Naomi is great. She's fun and energetic."

"Naomi Gray?" Brock asked from his spot by the door.

Clara turned in her seat. "Yeah. You know her too?"

Brock nodded. "She's sleeping with Susan and Geoff Tolbert behind each of their backs. It's actually been pretty crazy to watch for the past year."

"Seriously? Fuck. Why am I having such a tough time finding the right person?"

Probably because she had bad taste, but Caspian couldn't say that. "You need to open your mind to someone who might not be that exciting but who will treat you like a queen."

Clara nodded, looking thoughtful. "Okay. I'll think about it. Same time next week?"

Caspian smiled. "You're already on my calendar." They said their goodbyes while Caspian barely held on to his patience. Even after five months of dating,

Caspian never got enough of spending time with Brock. Brock had moved in with Caspian six weeks ago, and even so, Caspian wanted to quit his job to live like a mole stuck to Brock's back. He had never been this addicted to anyone. Brock was a sickness.

Brock waited until they were alone to focus a knowing smile on Caspian. "Jesus. She's really going to date the entire town before she gets to poor Scott."

Caspian snorted. "It's job security for me, so whatever. Do you have another case for me?"

Brock nodded. "I have a case of missing you with a huge side of being completely and sickening in love with you."

"Same," Caspian admitted, even as a part of him hid in fear. As much as he couldn't live without Brock, there was still a part of him hiding and Caspian hated it. Margo had said he would know when he had met the one, because his soulmate would accept him. He wasn't so sure Brock would accept that Caspian could do way more than simply see into the future.

Brock overcame him and kissed him. Caspian clung to the suit that perfectly molded Brock's body.

Brock's lips moved from Caspian's mouth to his ear. He licked. "You should do it just this one time."

"Do what?" Even to Caspian's ears, he sounded breathless.

"You should look into your future and prove to yourself that I'm your soulmate."

With his earlier potion still running through his veins, Brock's words conjured a vision with no permission from Caspian. He saw Brock and him together. They were laughing. Wedding rings adorned their fingers as they kissed.

"Stop conjuring plants. I'm the one who gets stuck watering them."

"I can't help it. My magic needs somewhere to go."

A gasp tore from Caspian. They were soulmates. Not only were they destined to marry, but Brock would also accept his magic and keep his secrets.

Brock's eyes danced with laughter. "I'm right, aren't I?"

"Yes."

Brock's smile faltered at the open shock in Caspian's voice. "Why do you sound like that? Aren't you happy being with me?"

At the hurt in Brock's voice, Caspian scrambled to set aside his surprise. He could muse over his vision later. Right now, the love of his life needed his reassurance. "Of course I'm happy with you. That's not what caught me off guard. We were married. I never dreamed you'd get up off your ass and propose."

A laugh burst from Brock. "Why do I have to be the one to propose? You're perfectly capable of asking."

Caspian's cheeks hurt from smiling. He had never been happier in his life. "Fine. You should marry me."

Brock snorted. "That's not a proposal." He unbuttoned his jacket and reached inside the inner pocket. As Brock came out with a ring, he dropped to one knee. "This is a proposal. Caspian Moonchild, will you marry me?"

Even as Caspian nodded in shock, he wondered what in the hell had happened to his life. Five short months ago, he had vowed to steer clear of any law enforcement. Now, he just agreed to marry an agent. Not only that, but he also couldn't wait to tie himself to this amazing man.

Brock kissed him. Things turned heated faster than usual. Caspian already had plans to lock the door and celebrate with a little multiple orgasms spell he had come to rely on a tad too much. Brock's cell-phone rang, interrupting them. With a growl, Brock pulled away and answered.

"Special Agent Brock Wray." His gaze moved to Caspian. He held Caspian's stare. "Yeah. I'm on my way." He stuffed his phone back inside his pocket. "Are you interested in a man-sized dog who walks on two legs and is eating everyone's cattle?"

Fuck. A werewolf. "Sure. I've got time."

With a smile, Brock pulled Caspian to his feet. "It's probably just a coyote or some other wild dog, but the strange and unusual is your specialty. Plus, it gives me an excuse to spend the day with you."

Caspian was all in. He would always accept any case that allowed him to steal more time with Brock. Plus, someone had to keep his man safe. No one watched

Brock's backside more thoroughly than Caspian. Caspian had seen their future, and it was beautiful. He would happily fight a werewolf for a shot at that life. There was nothing Caspian wouldn't do for Brock. There was nothing he wouldn't do for their love.

Introduction to Witchin Solstice

Special Agent Brock Wray is on the case of another weird crime. Strange enough to need the help of his warlock husband. This time, they can't do it alone.

After seven different men are found dead the same way—with zero clues pointing toward a killer—Brock has no choice but to get Caspian involved if he hopes to catch his perp. Each victim has the same final instructions on their computers. Directions on how to summon a monster lover. This calls for the help of a specialist. Luckily, Caspian knows just the guy.

As a supernatural detective, Titan has been on the hunt for one of his own for two years. It's his job to track and kill rogue members of certain species. Like him, most of his community has learned to live alongside humans without detection. Unfortunately, sometimes monsters give in to their true nature. When Titan arrives in the tiny town of Elvenwood, he never expects to find a human he can't resist working at the corner hardware store. Let's just hope he can keep the guy alive when there's a killer on the loose. One that his precious Jack will never see coming.

Witchin Solstice is the second book in Charity Parkerson's Witchin series. These fun, short paranormal romances are meant to be devoured on your lunch break. Read along as a tiny town in Ohio grows its supernatural community one resident at a time.

Chapter Five

THE STENCH of rotting flesh overcame Brock as he crossed the threshold of the newly renovated historic home on Maple. He immediately backed out again and put vapor rub beneath his nose before heading back inside. It wasn't a huge help, but it was enough to keep him in the home.

Brock bit back a sigh as he turned in a slow circle and eyed the walls. Tentacle dildos, dick-sucking octopuses, alien fists, and every other sex toy imaginable lined the shelves. That was why Brock was here. This was the seventh monster fucker found dead in the past two years. The extensive collection of strange toys and an online underworld of monster porn was the only thing connecting the deaths... oh, and they had all died of fright. Normally, stress cardiomyopathy didn't get the feds called in, but these cases were different. Each man died with similar instructions opened on their computers. Lube their asshole, bend over, and chant a spell. A snake-like man with a spiked cock would appear and fuck them. Considering each man had been sodomized by a spiky object shortly before death, there was a good chance they had a serial killer on their hands. At least, that was a normal agent's theory. Brock was married to Caspian, a true-blue warlock. Caspian had opened Brock's eyes to a whole new world of criminals: the supernatural community.

After a quick scan of each room and the body to ensure this was likely the same case, Brock headed back to his car and called Caspian. Caspian answered on the first ring.

"A client just left. I saw you calling."

Caspian ran a psychic business, but he wasn't an actual psychic. He used his magic to create a potion that allowed him to see the future.

Brock smiled. After seven months of marriage, Brock should have been at least a little less smitten with his sexy husband. Instead, his fascination grew every day. "Did you see why I'm calling?"

Caspian hummed. "Mhmm. How does one find that many dragon dildos?"

A bark of laughter burst from Brock. "I don't know. I'm afraid to have that on my browser history."

"I'm not."

A moment of heavy silence fell between them. A ragged-sounding breath brushed Brock's ear. "I'll get to searching. See you at home in an hour."

"I'm still working."

"You're about to take the rest of the day off."

Brock fought the urge to smile like an idiot. "Did you see that in your vision?"

"Yes."

Caspian's immediate answer had Brock's skin heating. "Then I'll see you in an hour."

"Good. I'll put some feelers out about the weird deaths. In the meantime..."

"Yeah. I'm coming."

A wicked-sounding chuckle caressed Brock's ear. "Damn right you are."

One of these days, Brock would lose his job over his inability to stay away from his new husband. Caspian was totally worth it.

Elvenwood, Ohio reeked of magic. Titan wasn't surprised they had been experiencing a ton of paranormal activity and monster-related deaths in and around the area. The town, and even those surrounding it, would lure supernatural beings by its scent alone. Titan was here for just one.

As the eldest living member of the Medusa bloodline, it fell to Titan to keep his species in line. He also investigated other paranormal crimes, but that was his profession. This hunt was personal and his responsibility. Seven men had already been found dead. Titan had to stop this before his fellow Gorgon exposed them all. The human investigators were already tossing around words like "monster." It was only a matter of time before they believed the term. Then no one in the paranormal community would be safe.

Despite the town's silent pulse of titillating magic, or maybe for that reason, Titan kind of liked the place's small-town feel. The tiny city made him feel like he had stepped back in time. A sense of nostalgia had him eyeing both sides of Main Street and fighting the urge to visit the corner pharmacy, even though he needed nothing from such a place to survive.

One of his connections out of New Orleans had pointed Titan toward a local psychic shop. According to the hours on the door, they should be open, but the doors were locked. Titan stepped to the side and searched the business online. He called the number listed. The phone rang four times before he was asked to leave a message. Titan blew out a sigh. It looked like he had some time to kill.

He jogged across the street to the diner. If he grabbed a table at the window, he could keep an eye out for the shop's owner to return. As he reached the door, it flew open and smacked him in the face before he could dodge it. His sunglasses went flying. Titan automatically squeezed his eyes shut and dropped to his haunches, searching. With his chin lowered, he peeked one eye open slightly, hoping to spot the spectacles before he killed anyone. It would be hard as hell to explain why random citizens were dropping dead around him.

"Oh no. I'm sorry. Who did I hit?"

A crunching sound had horror racing through him. Titan's gaze moved that way. A work boot-clad foot sat atop his favorite pair of sunglasses. The owner of the foot dropped to his haunches as well. He felt around his foot.

"Shit. What did I break?"

Titan's chin shot to the man's face without thinking. His gaze collided with the most beautiful blue eyes he had ever seen. The man stared directly at Titan. He didn't die.

"What did I break?"

Titan took a steadying breath. He couldn't as much as blink. Shock kept him frozen. "My sunglasses." And nearly his nose, but that didn't matter at the moment. Titan was completely struck dumb by the man's beauty.

The guy pulled a pair of sunglasses from his shirt pocket. "Here. Take mine. I'm so sorry. If you tell me your name and how to reach you, I'll get you a new pair."

On autopilot, Titan accepted the sunglasses and slipped them on before he made any more dumbass mistakes. His brain still reeled from the guy's undead state. He should have dropped like a stone the moment Titan looked at him with bare eyes.

"I'm Titan. Titan Braun. I'm just visiting, so..." Titan was too fascinated to think straight and decide where he was going with this rambling.

The man straightened.

So did Titan.

They cracked foreheads.

"Jesus." Titan rubbed his head.

The guy blushed. He looked truly horrified as he too massaged the place where they had collided. "Oh, my God. I'm so sorry. This really isn't my day. I'm usually not this much of a klutz." He bit his bottom lip, looking adorably rattled. His eyes faced Titan, but it was obvious he wasn't actually focused on Titan. It hit him. The man was blind.

"What's your name?" Titan had to know.

"Jack."

Titan smiled. "It's nice to meet you, Jack. And don't worry about the sunglasses. I have an extra pair back at the hotel."

Jack brightened. "Oh. Are you here visiting family?"

Someone tried exiting, but they blocked the door. Titan touched Jack's elbow and ushered him to the side as he answered. "Not family, no. I came to see the man who owns the psychic shop across the street, but he isn't there."

Jack nodded. "Caspian. Yeah. He's a great guy. Since he married Brock, you have to make an appointment to see him. He's always working a case with Brock or just still riding the newlywed high. Did you try their house?"

Titan couldn't stop staring at Jack's every nuance. His face was so animated. Titan had to shake his head to break the spell Jack weaved over him. "Not yet. I'd planned to go there next, but I forgot to write down his address. So I thought maybe I'd hang out here and watch for him to come back."

"Oh. Well, they live two doors down from me on Sycamore Street if you'd rather not wait around."

"If you have the exact address, that would make my life so much easier."

Jack brightened, as if he relished the idea of making Titan happy. "Sure. It's five seventeen Sycamore. You can walk there from here. It's pretty much right around the corner."

Titan knew their conversation was coming to an end. He felt oddly deflated at the knowledge. "Thank you. I'm glad we quite literally ran into each other."

"You have a nice voice." Jack blushed and scrambled to explain. "I just meant I don't recognize your accent, but I like it."

"I'm from Greece."

"Really?" Jack moved as if to touch Titan and immediately dropped his hand again. "I've always wanted to go there, but I'm also not very adventurous. Staying in my comfort zone, aka never leaving this town, is my limit, but still. I dream." A hint of sadness passed over Jack's features. Titan hated it.

Jack smiled. "Anyhow, I guess I should let you go find Caspian and I need to get back to work."

Titan took Jack's hand between his and lightly squeezed it. "It's been a pleasure, Jack."

For a moment, Jack didn't respond. Titan swore he could feel Jack soaking up the physical contact. Finally, he cleared his throat. "It has been. Hopefully, I'll run into you again. Maybe not so violently next time, but you get what I'm saying."

"I do and me too. Have a nice day, Jack."

"You too, Titan."

Titan watched Jack walk away. After a few steps, he pulled a collapsible white cane from his back pocket and headed down the sidewalk. Titan stared after him long enough that he worried he looked crazy. He forced himself to focus on something else. Titan pulled out his phone and searched for the address Jack had given him. Jack was right. It wasn't far away. Titan could easily walk from here. He put his phone away and headed out. Titan needed to find his prey. Then he had sunglasses to return.

Chapter Six

THE HOME BELONGING to Brock and Caspian Wray was a minuscule red-brick home with beautiful landscaping. Titan imagined it was the perfect size for a newlywed couple. He rang the doorbell, half expecting to be disappointed again. Movement stirred on the other side of the door almost immediately. When the door swung open, a man with tousled hair and brown eyes, wearing nothing but shorts, stared out at him. He looked barely awake for midafternoon.

"Hello," Titan said, sounding every bit as unsure of his timing as he felt. "I'm Titan Braun. I'm looking for Caspian Wray."

The guy eyed Titan for a moment before responding.

"You don't look like a Gorgon. I expected snake hair and to drop dead. Of course, the sunglasses make sense. I never would've expected such an easy fix."

Titan nodded. "Yeah. My kind would still live in caves, and you wouldn't have been able to call me for help if we hadn't embraced some modern advancements."

"I guess I sounded a little judgmental."

Titan bit back a smile. "A little."

A gorgeous smile stretched the guy's lips. "I'm Caspian. Come in."

With a nod, Titan stepped inside. Another man with dark blue eyes stepped into the living room from what looked to be the kitchen. He wore only pajama pants and chugged ice water. The hickies on his chest told the story, but some sort of childishness rose inside Titan.

"Did I wake you two?"

Caspian flashed a smile over his shoulder as he led Titan to the couch. "Nope. This is my husband, Brock," Caspian said, motioning the other man's way as he sat.

Titan nodded at Brock as he chose a nearby recliner. "Nice to meet you."

Caspian waited until after Brock filled the spot next to him and stole a kiss before continuing the introductions. "This is Titan Braun. When I called my New Orleans connection this morning, they said Titan was the man you needed to talk to about your case. I didn't know you'd get here this fast, though," Caspian added for Titan's sake.

Titan made a dismissive motion. "Actually, I was already headed this way when I got your call. I've been working the same case in the surrounding area for two years now."

Brock perked up at Titan's admission. "Really? I haven't heard of any other departments on the case. Who do you work for?"

"The Pantheon Council."

Brock blinked.

Titan flashed him a tight smile.

Caspian rubbed Brock's thigh. "He's sort of like a supernatural judge, jury, and executioner."

At Caspian's explanation, Brock's expression cleared. "Oh. Sorry. This is all still pretty new to me. When I fell hard for Caspian, I knew there was something special about him other than the obvious. But I'm still learning the ins and outs of your community."

Titan got it. The world was so much bigger than humans were taught. Mostly because they couldn't be trusted not to hunt, kill, and try to dominate everyone the least bit different from themselves. Occasionally, a good one came along. Brock seemed to fall into that category.

Brock set his water on the coffee table and visibly tried to shift into business mode. "So, who are we dealing with here and how do we catch him?"

Titan appreciated Brock's use of *who* and not *what* more than Brock would ever know. "His name is Bane Kratos, and *we* don't do anything. This one is on me. Any humans involved are as good as dead if they happen upon him. You'll never catch him."

Caspian jumped in, explaining on Titan's behalf. "Bane is a Gorgon: part of Medusa's bloodline."

A line appeared between Brock's eyebrows. "I thought Medusa turned people to stone."

"That's a myth, baby," Caspian said, patting Brock's knee.

Titan nodded. "In actuality, if I took these sunglasses off and looked at you, you'd drop dead."

"Stress Cardiomyopathy?"

Titan nodded.

"Just like our victims," Brock said, as if talking to himself. Then his focus zeroed in on Titan. "So you're one of these Gorgons too?"

Titan nodded again.

Brock's gaze moved down Titan's body. He swirled his finger through the air in Titan's direction as if he was hard pressed to figure out where exactly to point. "So you have a spiked dick?"

Caspian snorted.

A bark of laughter burst from Titan without thinking. "What?"

Brock looked completely serious. "The victims have all had internal damage from spiked penis penetration. In fact, it's what they signed up for. Each man followed a set of specific instructions to summon a monster lover before turning up dead."

Titan's humor fled. "I didn't know that. Since I'm not officially part of any of your government or police type agencies, I haven't been given access to the exact details of each case. I've just been following bodies and certain patterns."

"Like what?"

Since Brock seemed interested and Titan had come here to get information, he shared what he knew. "It's almost time for the solstice, which fires lots of supernatural hormones to life. Lots of breeding takes place this time of year."

"You mean, we're just getting a dump of dead bodies this time of year because your guy is horny?"

Titan shrugged. "To be fair, your victims are dead because they were horny too. Sounds like it went both ways."

Brock scoffed. "Yeah, but your guy isn't dropping dead. The humans are."

Ah. More prejudice. Titan was so glad he had signed up for this bullshit. "That's because *my guy* is a murderer. Something humans are also well known for being. At least I'm only hunting one killer. How many humans do you hunt each year?"

Brock held up his hand. "I recognize how I sound. I only meant no one should die for wanting sex."

Titan had to concede he was a little sensitive on the topic today. After all, he too was affected by the solstice, and he had run headlong into a man who had stared into Titan's soul with sightless eyes. Titan had resigned himself to always being alone outside of one-night stands. He had to spend too much effort to keep humans safe. But Jack hadn't been affected. Titan was a bit shaken. He wanted to see him again. "I understand, and I shouldn't have taken your words personally. We're on the same side."

The way Brock's shoulders visibly relaxed said a lot. "I could use the help."

That was true. Brock stood no chance of catching Bane without Titan. Except Titan's thoughts were now firmly locked on Jack, making it hard for him to focus. "What can you tell me about your neighbor, Jack?"

Caspian brightened. "Oh. That's a great idea. With Jack being gay and blind, he's the perfect person to use as bait... if he's willing, of course. I don't want to drag him into anything too crazy."

Titan hadn't been thinking that at all, but whatever it took to get more info on Caspian's sexy neighbor. Plus, Jack was gay. That was excellent news. "Yes. That's exactly what I was thinking." He did not sound like that was what he had been thinking, but Titan needed to know more. Specifically, he hoped to learn where to accidentally, on purpose, run into Jack again. "I met him outside the diner earlier and he pointed me in your direction after I found your shop closed."

Brock nodded, looking thoughtful. "Jack is pretty capable. He owns the hardware store on Main. If you'd like, I can talk to him and personally assure his safety."

Titan made a dismissive motion. "I'll talk to him. We should make some tentative plans, though. In case he agrees, don't you think?"

With a collective nod, they all sat forward and started plotting.

"We should set Jack up with a profile on the monster fuckers' website. That's where everything started with the other victims."

Caspian nodded at Brock's suggestion. "Agreed. I'll do it. I'm not scared of ending up on a list of perverts."

Titan nodded along, even though he had no clue what they were talking about. Only half of his brain followed their plan. The rest of Titan was already headed to the hardware store. He couldn't wait to see Jack again. He had to know why.

THE DAY MOVED FASTER than usual after Jack's wild encounter. As much as he loved living in a small town where he felt safe and could easily maneuver the city unhindered, it was nice meeting someone new. Heat filled his cheeks each time he thought about how much he had embarrassed himself. Yet Titan had been kind. He smiled as he thought of Titan's name. Titan Braun. So unusual. Jack liked it. Nothing ever changed in his life. Jack had been born here. He would likely die here. The worst part was, he would probably die alone. No one saw the gay, blind hardware store owner as anything other than a friend.

Jack blew out a sigh. It was what it was. For most people, it wasn't truly better to be safe than sorry. Jack wasn't one of those people. So he packed away his fantasies for real life. His watch alerted him of the time. Six p.m. meant closing time. Jack grabbed his keys and headed for the door. Before he reached it, the bell jingled, letting him know someone had come inside.

"I'm sorry. We just closed for the night."

"Oh. Okay. I just wanted to stop by and give back your sunglasses."

A smile exploded across Jack's face at the sound of Titan's voice. "Hey. You didn't have to do that. I owed you a pair."

He heard Titan shuffle closer. "Nah. I suffer from paralyzing migraines brought on by sunlight. I practically buy sunglasses in bulk to make sure I always have a pair."

"Well, I'm blind, so... same." Jack swore he heard Titan's smile.

"Quick question," Titan said, turning serious. "Who is Clara and why did she ask me if I'm her soulmate?"

A laugh burst from Jack. "You must have brown hair. Caspian told her that her soulmate has brown hair. Now she questions everyone whose hair is the least bit dark. Anyone with any sense could tell her it's the manager of the grocery store, Scott. The guy lives and breathes for her."

Titan chuckled. It was a nice sound. "Ah. That explains things."

Silence fell between them. Jack could practically feel Titan's reluctance to leave.

"So, um." Titan's voice moved closer. "Just so I don't keep searching for ways to see you if that's not what you want... am I crazy or is there a spark here?"

Damn. Jack really liked this guy. "That's refreshing. I don't meet many people who say what they mean."

Another sexy chuckle caressed Jack's ears. "You didn't answer me."

Heat crawled up Jack's face. He honestly didn't know what it was about Titan that made him so awkward. "Yeah. Sorry. No."

"Oh. I won't bother you again, then. Thanks for the sunglasses."

Jack's forehead furrowed. "Did I answer wrong? You asked me two different questions. No, you're not crazy. Yes, there's a spark. I wasn't trying—"

"May I take you to dinner?" Titan asked over Jack's rambling.

Jack took a breath, hoping to stop the idiocy. "I'd like that."

"Me too."

At Titan's confession, Jack's shoulders relaxed. "Okay. Lead the way." He heard the door open.

"Is the diner the only option here?"

Jack nodded and followed the sound of Titan's voice. "Pretty much." Jack went through his nightly routine of locking up while keeping up his end of the conversation. "There's a Dairy Queen at the edge of town and a pancake place that's open six to ten every morning. That's it. We're a pretty small community. In fact, people fought against the Dairy Queen when they first started talking about building the place. People were scared we'd suddenly be overrun with chain restaurants and local businesses would suffer."

Titan took his hand, surprising Jack. Jack didn't pull away. He simply held on and listened to the cadence of Titan's voice. "I understand. Where I'm from, everyone fears change. But it's a valid fear, sometimes. Your town has a quaint feel that makes me nostalgic. It could easily be destroyed if any corporations saw this place as the next gold mine."

They walked shoulder to shoulder with their fingers linked. Titan didn't rush. Jack savored every moment. Titan smelled exotic and alluring—like a newly discovered tropical fruit mixed with chocolate. Jack wanted to taste him.

"How long are you in town?"

Titan made a delicious humming sound. "I'm not sure. Caspian called me on Brock's behalf to consult on a case he's working. I suppose I'll be here until it's settled."

Jack tried not to be disappointed. He had known Titan was visiting from Greece. There was zero chance anything would come of this date. That didn't mean he wouldn't try to take things as far as he could. "So, are you like Greece's version of the FBI?"

"Something like that. How's the food at this diner?"

Since Jack understood Titan likely couldn't talk about this mysterious case, he let the change in topic stand. "It's pretty good. At least, I think it is. I haven't had much of a chance to make any comparisons. The farthest I've ever traveled is two counties over to Lockwood. It's not as easy for me to navigate the world as it is for others." Jack rethought his statement. "Or maybe I'm not as adventurous as I would like to be."

"You're taking a chance on a stranger. That's an adventure."

Pride filled Jack's chest at Titan's observation. "I suppose that's true. Not that it's a hardship, considering the company."

A sexy, deep chuckle rumbled from Titan. "Don't flatter me too much. I'm actually quite boring." He paused and squeezed Jack's hand. "I'm also very lucky you bothered with me after our collision this afternoon."

A smile played on Jack's lips. "What can I say? I'm fascinated."

"Me too."

The words brushed so closely to Jack's ear, there could be no doubt Titan stared at him. He prayed he didn't make an idiot of himself tonight and that Titan would see him again. As Titan had said, there was a spark. Jack wanted to keep feeling the heat. He was ready to get set ablaze.

Chapter Seven

THE DINER WAS PACKED with townsfolk. It shouldn't have surprised Titan, since Jack had warned it was pretty much the only restaurant in town. Still, Titan had hoped to have a bit more privacy. He didn't think he could convince Jack to invite him into his home after a couple of short encounters. He was still virtually a stranger. Jack didn't feel like one, though. Titan was oddly comfortable in Jack's company. He hoped Jack felt the same.

By the time they were seated, Titan felt like he had been introduced to a hundred people. He would never remember everyone's name. Jack impressed the hell out of him by how quickly he recognized everyone by voice alone. No one treated Jack any differently. That was refreshing as hell. As a member of a smaller species, Titan was accustomed to people being dismissive of anyone different from them. So far, this place wasn't like that. It warmed Titan's heart.

"What can I get you two to drink?"

"Hey, Debbie. I'll have my usual."

The buxom blonde turned Titan's way. "What about you, cutie?"

For a moment, Titan floundered. He thought it was obvious he was on a date, but then again, maybe not, and it was possible she wasn't flirting. Some people spoke like that to everyone. "Ice water is fine. Thank you."

"You got it, gorgeous."

As she walked away, a bright smile lit Jack's face. "Uh oh. It sounds like I have competition."

Damn. It was as Titan feared. "You absolutely do not."

Two drinks appeared in front of them.

Debbie openly eyed him. "So, where did you come from? I would remember if I'd seen someone who looks like you around town."

"Greece."

The blonde pursed her lips and openly eyed Titan's body. "Mhmm. Nice. Do you guys wear deodorant over there?"

Jack ducked his head, but not before Titan saw his silent laughter.

Debbie didn't give him time to answer. She leaned closer, making sure he got a face full of half exposed breasts. "I mean, you smell pretty good to me."

"Um. Thanks."

"You should take off those sunglasses and let see your eyes. I bet they're gorgeous."

"Order eleven up."

Debbie glanced over her shoulder at the shout. She blindly patted Titan's shoulder. "I'll be right back, sugar."

The moment she walked away, Titan snagged his drink and stood. "We have to nip this in the bud. Scoot over."

Jack dutifully slid deeper into the booth, making room for Titan. After filling the space next to Jack, he took Jack's hand and held it on the table where their linked fingers wouldn't be missed. "There."

"She's very nice." Heavy laughter laced Jack's claim.

"I'm sure that's true, but I'm here with you."

The humor slipped from Jack's expression. Hunger took its place. Titan couldn't look away. In all his years, he had seen no one more beautiful.

Jack licked his lips, looking nervous. "Where did you even come from? It seems so farfetched to think everything I've ever wanted just dropped into my lap on a Tuesday."

Titan felt like he was falling into Jack's eyes. He was living proof there was someone for everyone. It was humbling when Titan had always expected to be alone.

"What can I get you two to eat?"

Titan tore his gaze away from Jack to focus on Debbie. If she had any thoughts on his shift in positions, he couldn't tell. She stopped flirting, and that was all he cared about.

"I forgot to look at the menu."

"We'll have the special," Jack said, ordering for them.

Debbie nodded and moved along.

Jack stroked his hand. "Trust me. You'll like it, and this way, we'll have fewer interruptions."

Titan leaned closer. He liked this plan. The food wasn't important anyhow. Titan was here for Jack. He needed all the alone time he could get.

JACK HADN'T KNOWN what to expect out of dinner, but Titan, being so proud to be with him, had been fucking incredible. Titan walked him home and all the way to the front door. Jack didn't want the night to end. After a single dinner, he felt comfortable in Titan's company. The guy was perfect. He treated Jack with such care and acted as if they had known each other their entire lives. It was nice.

As they moved up the front steps of Jack's house, his nerves set in. He wanted Titan to kiss him. But it had been years since anyone kissed him and Jack wondered if he even remembered how. He knew it was a pathetic fear. His worries were real, nonetheless.

"This was nice. Thank you for dinner."

"It was. Hopefully, you'll let me see you again."

Jack bit his bottom lip, trying to squelch a ridiculous smile at Titan's words. "I'd like that."

He felt Titan shuffle closer. Jack held his breath. "Maybe you could show me the pancake house in the morning."

For a moment, Jack scrambled to decide if he was being asked to breakfast, or if Titan asked to stay the night. He didn't respond.

"I don't know if that place is within walking distance, but I could stop by in the morning, and we could figure it out."

Relief washed over Jack at Titan's clarification. Not that Jack didn't want to invite Titan inside. He was already nervous as hell over a kiss. Jack couldn't imagine how big of a wreck he would be for sex. "That sounds great, and yeah. It's within walking distance."

He felt Titan move even closer. Jack's heart rate kicked up. Titan stroked his arm from shoulder to elbow. "Would it be okay if I kissed you?"

He was such a gentleman—like almost old-world respectful. Jack could barely breathe from the neediness that overcame him. "I'd like that."

Titan's fingers skimmed across Jack's jaw. His touch was cool and made goosebumps rise on Jack's skin. Jack gingerly reached for Titan. His hands found Titan's waist. His breath caught at the first real feel of Titan's trim body. He didn't know what Titan looked like, but he obviously drew people to him, and he felt fucking amazing beneath Jack's hands. Titan kept moving until his breath fanned Jack's face. His cool lips barely skimmed Jack's mouth when the sound of breaking glass sent Jack's heart racing into his throat. Titan moved so fast, Jack had a hard time keeping up. In a matter of less than a second, Jack clung to Titan's hard shoulders. It took him a moment to realize Titan had shoved him behind his back.

"Someone is in your house."

Jack's anxiety skyrocketed. Someone breaking into his home was one of Jack's top five fears. It was one of the main reasons he stayed in Elvenwood. Without his sight, he knew strangers would target him. The last thing he wanted was to be scared in the only town he knew.

"Oh, my god. What do I do? I should call Wade."

"Who is Wade?"

Damned if Titan didn't sound jealous. It was hot, even under the worst of circumstances. "He's the guy who works nights at the police station."

Titan scoffed. "You don't need Wade. You have me."

Thank goodness, because he didn't know how long it would take Wade to get here. Jack needed help right now. "Right. Greece's version of the FBI. Got it. Do you carry guns in Greece?"

Titan snorted. "I don't need a gun. Wait here."

Jack's fingers refused to unclench from Titan's shoulders.

Titan pried them loose. "Seriously. Stay put."

Jack forced himself to let go. His nerves nearly shattered as Titan stepped away. "Do you need my key?"

The screen door squeaked open.

"No. The door is open about half an inch."

Shit. Jack clenched his jaw when his teeth chattered at Titan's whispered claim. He felt helpless. A loud grunt rent the air. Feet shuffled. He heard blows landing and an exchange of angry words that sounded hissed. Jack bolted. His feet moved without his brain's permission. He automatically followed the familiar path down the sidewalk until he felt the second dip in the pavement that showed he had made it two doors down. Jack tripped and scrambled back upright before making it up the front steps. He blindly searched for the doorbell before banging on the door.

A breeze hit his skin as the door flew open beneath his fist.

Jack didn't wait to check who answered. "There's someone in my house. I think he jumped Titan."

"Stay here." A body quickly moved past him before a gentle hand touched his arm.

"Come on," Caspian said, sounding determined when Jack immediately moved to follow Brock. "I'll go with you."

Jack's entire body shook with fear and adrenaline. He let Caspian help him back home. Normally, he was pretty good at navigating the town he had memorized over the years, but he was too scared to think.

When they reached his front porch again, all Jack heard was panting.

"Who's hurt. What's happening?"

Caspian let go of Jack's arm. His footsteps slapped the ground as he ran away. Jack wanted to scream. He needed answers. Just when he thought he would snap, strong hands caressed his body.

"Are you okay? What happened? You're bleeding."

Jack nearly collapsed in his relief as Titan worried over him. "I'm fine. I fell, rushing to get Brock and Caspian, and skinned my hand. What happened? Who's in my house?"

Titan made a soothing sound. "It's okay. Take a breath. Brock and I have everything under control. It was the guy I came to town to find."

Jack's throat swelled with fear. "He was here. Did you catch him? Where is he?" Even Jack heard the fear in his voice. He couldn't stop. If he had been alone, he might be dead already. This was his home. Now it didn't feel safe. He couldn't breathe. His head spun. He might never feel safe again.

EACH SECOND THAT PASSED, Jack looked closer to fainting. Titan cast a look Brock's way. They both dropped their gazes to the dead Gorgon on Jack's living room floor. Caspian, Brock, and he exchanged glances. They could not let Jack know. Jack was already visibly at the edge of what he could handle. Titan expected he would hyperventilate any second. He couldn't let that happen.

Titan gathered Jack into his arms. "Don't worry. Brock showed up just in time. You did great. Brock has him in custody. You have nothing to fear."

Caspian pulled a pained face as he stepped over the pool of black blood staining Jack's hardwood. He grabbed a throw blanket from the back of the couch and passed it Titan's way. He wrapped a shaking Jack in the blanket and led him to a rocking chair on the front porch.

"Everything is over now. Please just sit here and let us get this guy out of here. Then I promise I will thoroughly inspect this place and make sure you're a hundred percent safe."

Jack nodded. His face was pale. "Okay. I just don't understand why he was here."

Titan felt guilty as hell. He honestly couldn't imagine Jack having his security ripped away. It was obvious he relied heavily on the familiar to navigate the world. Titan would be his eyes and safety net.

"There's no telling with psychopaths," Titan said, hoping to soothe his fears. After ensuring Jack was settled, Titan headed inside. He closed the door half-way, hoping to hide the grisly scene inside from any nosy neighbors. Titan also hoped to muffle their whispered conversation.

"What did you use to take off his head? I need to destroy that too," Caspian whispered.

Titan held up his hands.

Caspian's jaw dropped. "You ripped off his head with your bare hands?"

Titan shrugged. "I was angry. He was in Jack's house. Why didn't you warn me you were setting up Jack's profile on that site tonight?"

"We need to get rid of this body before anyone sees," Brock whispered, cutting in.

Caspian nodded. He swirled his hands through the air until a green light grew. The air crackled and popped with a powerful energy. Caspian's eyes glowed green as the power flowed through him. As Titan looked on, the body and mess became engulfed in magic and vanished.

"That's impressive."

At Titan's compliment, Caspian flashed him a smile. "Thanks. Also, I haven't set up Jack's profile yet. I was waiting for you to give me the green light."

They exchanged glances again.

Brock said what they were all thinking. "Why was he here, then? What drew him to Jack?"

"Is Jack into monster cock?"

"Am I into what?" Jack screeched, bringing all eyes toward the open doorway. With the blanket wrapped around him and looking pale as fuck, Jack stood waiting for answers.

Titan winced.

Caspian scrambled to explain his insane question. "Shit. Sorry. That sounded awful. The FBI thinks the guy Titan just busted in your house has been finding his victims through a chat room for men who like monster cocks. Jesus," Caspian muttered under his breath. "That really didn't make my question sound any better."

Jack blinked several times, as if he had unexpectedly been slapped across his face. He cleared his throat. "Um. Yeah. I can't say I've been hanging out in any monster cock chat rooms."

Titan rubbed his forehead. He couldn't believe this was happening.

"Huh."

All eyes turned Jack's way at his thoughtful sound.

"I do subscribe to this one podcast, though. This guy tells these lurid tales of a monster serial killer who stalks these men online. He sets the men up to have sex with him and then kills them. It's kind of a fantasy crime podcast."

"What the guy's name?"

"Bane Kratos."

Titan shook his head. He couldn't believe something so obvious could have led him to Bane before now. He had been too busy hunting Bane like a monster. It had never occurred to Titan that Bane might find his victims through the most modern of means. His victims found him. They literally signed up to be murdered. "That's the guy."

Jack clutched the blanket tighter. "You mean his stories were real?"

Titan winced. "In a manner of speaking."

Jack's shoulders visibly squared. "I'm glad you caught him, then. Where is he?"

Brock, Caspian, and Titan exchanged glances again. Caspian was the quickest to find a lie. "Titan knocked him out. Brock is getting ready to take him in. We'll just do that and get out of your hair."

Jack moved farther into the room, making room for them to pass. "Do I need to make a statement or anything like that?"

"That's unnecessary," Brock assured him. "We have plenty of evidence against the guy. I'm just thankful Titan was here."

Jack nodded.

Titan saw Caspian and Brock out. As Caspian passed Titan, he brushed a glowing hand over Titan's body, removing all signs of Bane's blood. Titan flashed him a grateful smile before closing the door behind the pair. He turned to find Jack standing in the middle of his living room, looking lost. Titan's heart squeezed in his chest. He took off his sunglasses and squeezed the spot between his eyes where a pain bloomed. Titan set the glasses aside to focus on Jack. For a moment, he was stricken speech-less. He had forgotten what it was like to look upon anyone with his bare eyes. Color seemed so much more vibrant. His eyesight was more heightened than a human's. He could see clearly through sunglasses no matter the time of day or night, but there was just something about getting to look at Jack with no danger of harming him. It was nice. He didn't have to be on guard every second.

"You saved my life."

Titan's throat swelled. Thank God he had been here. He couldn't have known Jack was next on Bane's list. There hadn't been the same prep on Jack's part as the other victims. Bane had broken pattern to come after Jack. Titan could only assume, the closer the solstice came, the more desperate and sloppier Bane had become. Jack was blind. He wouldn't have dropped dead like the others. Bane might have done anything when he realized Jack wouldn't die peacefully. He might have murdered him horribly, or worse. Bane could have chosen to keep Jack as some sort of sex slave. The horrible possibilities were endless. Determination filled Titan. He would keep Jack safe.

"I would never let anything happen to you."

A sweet smile touched Jack's lips and warmed Titan's heart. "This has definitely been the craziest date I've ever had."

Titan chuckled. "One for the record books, really."

Jack bit his bottom lip. A snort escaped him a half second before he roared with laughter. "Caspian asked you if I was into monster cock." Jack choked out the words between guffaws. His eyes swam with laughter. Jack tried covering his mouth and stifling the sounds he made.

Titan couldn't look away. "You're beautiful."

Jack's laughter died. His expression turned hungry. They moved at the same time, meeting in the middle. Titan claimed Jack's mouth. Jack's hands were everywhere. Logically, Titan understood Jack saw through touch, but he had Titan's body on fire. Jack's kiss was hungry, as if he was every bit as starved for affection as Titan. Titan caught himself kneading Jack's ass, but he couldn't stop. The needy sounds Jack made drove him.

Jack's hands found the button on Titan's jeans. His pants loosened.

Titan rallied. "Wait. I have to tell you something."

Jack's mouth moved to Titan's throat. "I'm listening."

"I'm a Gorgon."

Jack tried pushing Titan's jeans down his hips without much luck. "Cool."

Titan knew Jack wasn't really listening, but he kept trying. "I'm a descendant of Medusa. That's the real reason I wear sunglasses everywhere."

"Don't care," Jack said as he pulled his shirt up and over his head before tossing it aside.

Titan eyed Jack's half nude body. His dark hair was already a mess. The same dark hair covered his chest. Titan's mouth watered at just the sight of him. "Good enough for me. Which direction is the bedroom?"

Jack pointed toward an open door on the left.

Titan swept Jack into his arms and headed that way.

"Holy shit." Jack scrambled to hold on to Titan's neck. "Good God. We're the same size. You're fucking strong as hell."

"Descendant of Medusa," Titan reminded him as he set Jack on the edge of the bed.

Jack looked thoughtful for a moment. "You're serious, aren't you?"

Titan kicked off his shoes and peeled off his shirt. "Yep."

Jack fell backward and went to work on his jeans. "You'll have to tell me about that someday."

Even though Titan didn't understand why Jack took things so in stride, he wasn't looking a gift horse in the mouth. If Jack freaked out later, he would cross that bridge when he got there. For now, he wanted to taste the man waiting for him. He grabbed the condom and travel size lube from his wallet before stripping away the rest of his clothes. Jack looked cold. Titan needed to warm him. He kissed Jack's stomach as he crawled onto the mattress. Jack cupped his head and drew Titan up his body until he could reclaim Titan's mouth.

"I love the way your tongue feels," Jack whispered between kisses.

"Gorgon," Titan reminded him as he urged Jack's thighs apart.

"Is that all that's different about you?"

It hit Titan. Jack wasn't totally distracted by arousal. He believed. There were only small differences between his body and a human's if he didn't count his strength and ability to kill with a glance. But without his sight, Jack could likely feel those differences more than a normal human.

Titan leaned away a hair. "My skin is colder than a human's." He took Jack's hand and led it down his body. "And softer," he added as he urged Jack to touch his dick.

Jack's fingers encircled Titan's erection. He stroked, making Titan pant. "Damn. That is nice. I noticed your skin felt cool to the touch. I wonder how hot I'll feel to you when you're buried inside me."

Titan's stomach cramped. Jack was perfect. He wasn't scared, and he didn't think Titan was crazy. Titan didn't have to hide his eyes or anything about himself. He had never felt this free. "Let's find out." Titan went to work, lubing Jack's asshole while Jack openly writhed beneath his touch. "I'm impatient for you," Titan confessed as he rolled the condom down his length. "That's the only reason I'm rushing, but I promise I'll make it better later. I'll show you what this tongue can really do."

Jack moaned, as if he already knew.

Titan took advantage of the distraction and impaled Jack.

Jack gasped.

Titan held still, trying to give him time to adjust. When Jack's short fingernails scored Titan's skin, Titan lost control. He pulled out slightly and impaled Jack again.

"Yes. Please. You have no idea how much I want it."

Jack didn't need to beg or explain. Titan felt the same. Other than the occasional quick tryst, Titan didn't have this in his life. Jack struck him as the same. "Don't worry, sexy. I have all the time in the world, and I can give it to you." Titan settled in, taking his time as he thrust inside Jack. Jack squirmed and fought to get closer. He open-mouth gasped for air as Titan ensured his every thrust hit at the perfect angle. When Jack's muscles tensed, Titan held his breath. Jack cried out. Cum coated Jack's stomach as his body tried sucking Titan deeper.

A growl ripped from Titan. His pace quickened. He slammed into Jack over and over. "That's it, baby. I'm eating that cum after I've ruined this ass. You're so goddamn tight and hot on my dick. I can't get enough."

Jack's cries still reverberated from the walls when an orgasm slammed into Titan, stealing his soul. He sucked Jack's bottom lip, stifling the sounds tearing from his throat. Titan swore he came forever. The wildness didn't leave him. He felt primal in that moment, and the truth overwhelmed him. Titan had found his mate. That was why Jack wasn't scared. His family had always said a true mate wouldn't fear them and would make them burn hotter than the sun in their possessiveness. Titan got it now. Jack was the one for him. He had found his home.

***

JACK LISTENED to Titan's steady heartbeat and reveled in the way his body ached in all the best ways. A small part of him recognized he should likely freak out over Titan's claims. Jack couldn't explain why he wasn't surprised. He thought it might be his blindness. Jack's lack of sight forced him to see things in a different way, and he was more attuned to his surroundings. There was something about Elvenwood.

When Jack made trips to the surroundings towns, the air changed. It turned duller. He always knew when he was close to returning home. The air sizzled and popped with life here. Titan's claim not only gave credence to Jack's feelings, but it also brought back stories his grandmother used to tell him about Elvenwood. His grandmother claimed Elvenwood was just that: the Elven's woods. Everything here was surrounded by magic and the scent drew creatures here. She claimed everything people dismissed as fairytales were actually brushed aside from history. His mom always fussed that Granny filled his head with nonsense. Granny would always scoff and tell Jack to just wait. She had sworn something special was meant for Jack. Someone special. Jack supposed, in the back of his mind, he had always believed. Then Titan had turned up in his life, and Jack felt the truth in his gut. Titan was special. Or maybe Titan was crazy and what difference did that make anyhow?

Everyone was a little insane. He was too happy to care.

"I like this little town."

Jack smiled against Titan's chest. "Based on the way everyone's taken to you, I'd say this little town likes you too."

"I also really like you."

Jack pressed his lips together, trying to beat back the happiness that grew inside him by the second.

"My case is over now, but I don't want to leave."

Jack's happiness disappeared. He hadn't thought about that. Titan didn't live in the US. Jack had to be as honest as Titan had been. "I don't want you to leave either. There's something here. Between us," he clarified.

Titan kissed his forehead. Silence grew between them, and tension built in Jack's chest. He didn't want to lose Titan. He didn't know how to stop it from happening. After a moment, he felt Titan's chest expand on a deep breath. "I'll find a way to stay."

With that one claim, relief poured through Jack. He didn't know how Titan could possibly pull off that feat, but he knew Titan would. It was a little crazy how much Jack believed in Titan in such a short time. He just felt in his soul they were meant for more.

"I have faith."

Titan rolled, pinning Jack beneath him. His lips skimmed the corner of Jack's mouth before his tongue flicked out with the lightest of brushes, setting Jack's skin ablaze. "And I have faith you can come again for me."

Jack wasn't as sure about that one. Titan had already tested the lengths of his body. He was willing to try, though. In fact, there was nothing Jack wasn't willing to do as long as Titan stayed. Jack would believe any wild story. Turn his life upside down. Whatever it took, Jack was in. This was the life for him. He wanted this.

Chapter Eight

WHILE WORKING for the Pantheon Council still meant Titan traveled for work, he spent less time away from Jack all the time. He had moved in six months ago, after the Pantheon had decided a true mate was a worthy enough reason to stay and work full-time in the US. Titan had been in Texas for a week, hunting, and had gotten home only ten minutes ago. He dropped his bags and immediately headed for the hardware store.

Even though Titan knew he would be better off getting some rest before the store closed, he didn't have the patience to wait. He needed to see Jack. Several people stopped him along the way, testing his patience as they asked about his trip. As much as

Titan had fallen in love with this town, he wanted Jack. By the time he reached the store, he was ready to run inside. Instead, he nodded at Hank—the local liquor store owner—as he held the door open for the man to go inside ahead of him. Then he only had eyes for Jack.

Jack turned toward the sound of the jingling bell. "Good afternoon. How can I help you?"

A bright smile stretched Titan's lips as he headed Jack's way. "You can kiss me hello."

The love that lit Jack's features always punched Titan in the chest. Jack immediately walked into Titan's arms and kissed him like he hadn't seen him in a year.

"You should close up early," Titan whispered between kisses.

Jack nipped at Titan's bottom lip. "Should I? Did you bring that monster cock home hungry?"

"I'll come back later."

Jack froze at Hank's words. The door jingled again at Hank's exit. Jack dropped his forehead to Titan's shoulder and shook with silent laughter.

"Oh, my God. I didn't hear him come in. I thought we were alone."

Titan's face hurt from smiling. He never got enough of Jack's blushes. "We are now."

Jack's laughter died away. His expression went through a myriad of emotions before landing on aroused. "Quick. Lock the door before anyone else comes in."

Titan didn't need to be told twice. He quickly turned the lock and returned to Jack's arms. As their lips met again, Titan realized this was exactly why he hadn't waited at home. Every second with Jack was explosive and addictive. He couldn't get enough. Not only that, but he had known Jack would put him above everything else. Just as he had from the moment they met, and Jack had given up his sunglasses for Titan. Even though death had led him here, Titan didn't doubt for a moment fate had actually been the person in charge. Sometimes, he wondered if that particular deity was a bit of a voyeur. As Jack lured Titan toward the back of the store while working on divesting Titan of his clothes, he was sure that was the case. His life and the passion he shared with Jack was unmatched.

Titan held Jack still for a moment. He had something he needed to say. "I love you."

Jack visibly melted. "I love you too."

"We should get married."

Jack's features went slack with shock before the purest of happiness overcame his expression. "We definitely should."

Titan smiled. He stared at Jack while love welled inside him until it nearly overflowed.

"We should fuck first."

Jack's claim shook Titan from his frozen reverence. "Oh, yeah. Definitely. We should do that."

For a moment, neither of them budged before they burst into laughter. Titan knew it was their happiness overflowing. They had found so much joy in each other, sometimes it had nowhere to go. As Jack pulled Titan back in for a kiss, Titan made a silent vow. It would always be this way. For the rest of their lives, he would cherish this blessing. If fate was a voyeur, he would give her one hell of a show. He would be worthy of this love. He would be worthy of Jack.

Introduction to Witchin Moonbeam

THERE'S ANOTHER MYSTERY IN
ELVENWOOD. THIS TIME, THE POLICE
ARE ON THE CASE. IT'S NOT GOING
WELL.

For all of his adult life, Wade has worked the night shift for the Elvenwood police department. It's an easy gig with only the occasional burst of excitement. Either nothing happens in his town or it's a case too big for the local police. Mostly, Wade just kills time on the clock. Now, people's pets are going missing in droves. As a huge dog lover, that's something that doesn't sit right with Wade. He has to figure this one out.

With zero clues, Wade heads to the local psychic, hoping Caspian might see something he can't. Instead, Wade realizes the answer is a lot closer to home than he thinks, and he has a much bigger problem than he ever dreamed.

Witchin Moonbeam is the third book in Charity Parkerson's Witchin series. These fun, short paranormal romances are meant to be devoured on your lunch break. Read along as a tiny town in Ohio grows its supernatural community one resident at a time.

Chapter Nine

WORDS BLURRED WITH NO MEANING. Wade stared at his book, seeing nothing. All the weird crimes as of late weighed heavily on his mind. He was just a small-town cop. Wade wasn't some big-city detective. He was just one of eight police officers in the tiny community of Elvenwood. Three of those were reserve officers in case of illness or emergency. But Elvenwood was his home, and he cared about its people. The town was his responsibility. People around these parts got pretty upset when their pets went missing. He understood. Wade wished he could do more. If there had been any signs of coyotes, Wade would feel slightly better about the disappearances. Obviously, that would still be horrible. But if they had some wild animals running off with domestics, then Wade could call someone in from wildlife to help, but no. The only tracks he had seen were human. That either meant nothing or something bad. He didn't know which, and that bothered him.

Charlie perked up, as if he sensed Wade's worry. He licked Wade's toes, going all the way in. Wade chuckled as the prickly tongue swiped between his toes.

He set his book aside and glanced down the line of his body at the huge, white wolfdog licking his feet. "Are you having fun?"

Charlie paused.

Wade swore the dog smiled at him before going back to taste all of Wade's foot.

Wade shook his head. "You can't just let a man relax, can you? Every time I stretch out on this couch, your foot fetish gets the best of you. You know that's gross, right? Lucky for you, I haven't had a foot massage in ages. That's the only reason I'm letting this go on."

Wade watched the giant fur monster a second longer before giving in. "Fine. Come here."

Charlie immediately pounced, jumping onto the couch, and crawling all over Wade, nearly knocking the wind from Wade with his weight, before finding a comfy spot half on Wade's chest and half squashed against the couch.

"There's no way you're comfortable."

Charlie huffed.

Wade rolled his eyes. "Well, I'm not. You weigh as much as I do."

Charlie licked his face.

Wade ran his fingers through Charlie's fur and scratched his head. "I love you too."

With Charlie's body cuddled against him and his rapid heart beating against Wade's chest, Wade closed his eyes and snuggled closer to his best friend. He had adopted Charlie a year ago from a local shelter after Charlie bit him as a stray. After his ten days of observation for rabies ended, Wade couldn't let him be put down. It had been Wade's fault. He had been trying to catch the stray when he spooked him. Wade had a soft spot for the beast. He was gigantic and obviously more wolf than dog, but he was beautiful and incredibly sweet once he got to know Wade. It would break Wade's heart if Charlie turned up missing like a few of the dogs in town. More than a few. It was like an epidemic. He needed to figure this out.

Wade kissed Charlie's head. Charlie had never been much of an outdoor dog, despite his breed and large size. Once Wade had let him inside, he hadn't gotten Charlie to sleep outdoors again. Wade was glad for that now. He didn't know what was going on with the township, but he would look into it a little harder the first chance he got. Hell, maybe he would go talk to the local psychic, since everyone else believed in the guy. Wade didn't put much stock in things he couldn't see, but it couldn't hurt to get another opinion. He kissed Charlie again. A wave of exhaustion washed over him. Wade closed his eyes and rubbed Charlie's back. He would get started tomorrow. There was no time like the present.

Charlie listened to Wade's heartbeat and breathing. He waited until he knew Wade was out for the count before slipping to the floor. As his back paws hit the hardwood, Charlie's body transformed. He checked Wade's breathing then went hunting for his jeans. He always hid them either behind the dryer or the couch, depending on where he changed forms. Charlie checked the dryer first. He nearly sighed when he found them. Charlie hated to spend too much time tiptoeing around Wade's sleeping form, but he had things to do.

Once sufficiently dressed, Charlie went through his nightly routine. He checked the perimeter of the house, ensuring the place was secure before heading back to the kitchen. First, he dumped the disgusting dog food Wade bought. Then he ate Wade's leftovers. It wasn't ideal, but Charlie would be damned if he ate dog food. Wade's heart was in the right place. He bought the best dog food on the market. But Charlie was a goddamn werewolf. Puppy Chow wouldn't cut it. He needed meat.

After devouring what he could without raising suspicion, Charlie headed for the bathroom. He found the toothbrush he kept hidden at the back of the drawer and brushed his teeth as quietly as possible. Wade slept like the dead, but Charlie had to get his showers while Wade was at work. There was no way he could risk taking one with Wade home. Nonetheless, he tried to clean up as much as possible before returning to his dog form.

With his nightly routine out of the way, he trotted to Wade's side and went back to licking his feet. Wade was right. Charlie had a foot fetish, but this was also the least jarring way to get Wade's attention. Wade was a cranky bastard when startled awake.

Wade rolled and peeked one eye open. He groaned and eyed the clock. "I take it you're ready for bed."

Charlie headed for the bedroom and leaped onto the bed. He knew Wade would follow. He settled in and watched as Wade stripped down to his underwear. Love filled Charlie's chest. Wade had given him a home and loved him, even though Charlie had bitten him the first time they met. They were a family. Sometimes, Charlie desperately wanted to show himself to Wade, but he knew Wade would lose his shit. Charlie had nowhere else to go. So he took what he could get. Any form of Wade's affection was better than none. Charlie was mostly content.

Wade pulled back the covers. Charlie crawled beneath them while Wade turned off the lights. As Wade climbed in next to Charlie and cuddled close,

Charlie's heart broke a little. He would always be Wade's beloved pet and nothing more, really. Sometimes he dreamed, though. Charlie's life had been nothing but longing for something real since the day he was born. That was the way things would always be. He had to accept his fate.

Chapter Ten

The MINUSCULE PSYCHIC shop on Main was part of a larger strip of stores. By larger, Wade meant like six stores. Everything a person could possibly need could be found on Main and most homes were within walking distance. Quite a few people worked in one of the larger surrounding cities, so people did own cars here, but they rarely used them during the summer months while only navigating Elvenwood. It was easier to traverse the town on foot.

Wade wasn't technically on duty. His shift didn't start until three thirty. But he had to take Charlie for a walk anyhow, so he took a chance Caspian could fit him in for some advice. He stood outside Futures Untold for five minutes, trying to decide if Caspian would care if he brought Charlie inside. Finally, he gave up and walked Charlie through the door as if he had every right to be there. With everything going on, he would be damned if he left Charlie outside unattended.

His neighbor, Clara, gathered her things to leave as he stepped inside. Wade was half convinced Clara lived at Caspian's shop, and one hundred percent certain she solely kept Caspian in business. She flashed Wade a smile and rubbed Charlie's head on her way out the door. Clara was a good one. Her biggest fault was loneliness, but Wade got it. The hardest thing about a small town was meeting someone new. God knew everyone else knew too much about each other to want to date anyone.

Caspian's sweet brown gaze moved Wade's way. He eyed Charlie but didn't demand Wade take him outside, as Wade had feared he would. "Officer Deerman. What brings you by today?"

Honestly, Wade didn't know where to start. Unfortunately, his tongue had a mind of its own. "You mean you didn't see me coming?" A nervous chuckle followed his dumbass comment. Wade tried to reel it in. "Sorry. Bad joke. I'm sure you hear it all the time."

Caspian smiled. "It's fine. You get accustomed to some things when you're like me." His gaze moved back to Charlie again, as if he couldn't stop looking at him. "You have a gorgeous... dog. He gets bigger every time I see him. Were you ever able to get him neutered?"

Charlie growled.

Caspian flashed the dog a wry look and chuckled.

Wade shifted nervously. Charlie never growled at anyone. He swore they understood each other. "No. He keeps escaping the vet's office and finding his way home before they can do the surgery."

Caspian hummed. "Maybe best to leave him alone then. He doesn't look like the type to roam."

Wade swore Charlie gave Caspian a sharp nod before settling down to rest on top of Wade's feet. He tried to steer the conversation toward the reason he was there. "Yeah, speaking of roaming pets. That's why I stopped by. Quite a few of the townsfolk's pets have gone missing. There're no signs of wild animals carrying them off, and frankly, I'm stumped. I wondered if you could help." He felt dumb as hell. "You know, maybe see something. With your third eye or whatever," Wade finished lamely.

A kind smile touched Caspian's lips, stealing some of Wade's awkwardness. "Sure. If you can bring me a collar or something that belongs to one of the missing animals, I'd be glad to try."

Wade nodded. "Sure. I can do that. I'll stop by Hank's place and see if he'll loan me one of his cat's many collars. You know how he had a million different outfits and whatnot for Princess."

Caspian pulled a pained face. "Oh no. I hadn't realized he lost Princess. I'm sure he's crushed."

Wade nodded and eased toward the door. He liked Caspian, but Wade wasn't much on socializing. He had spent more energy on chatting than usual. His anxiety spiked a little higher by the second. Charlie pressed against his shins as if he felt Wade's blood pressure rising.

"Thanks again for your help. I'll stop back by in the next few days."

Caspian's gaze moved to Charlie again. "It's no problem. Whatever I can do to keep people safe." Caspian never looked away from Charlie as he made the claim.

Charlie ushered him toward the door. Wade gave a final wave goodbye before stepping out. He glanced down at Charlie and shook his head.

"Damn, boy. I know I'm an anxiety-ridden mess, but I can find my own way out the door."

Charlie trotted along, ignoring him.

Wade shook his head. He didn't know if Caspian could actually help, but he felt a little better anyhow. At least he wasn't sitting on his hands. Maybe he would crack this case after all. Stranger things had happened.

CHARLIE'S MIND raced as they headed home. He couldn't let Wade go through with searching for the lost animals in town. Wade was not ready to find those answers. Even though Charlie had feared it was only a matter of time before Wade figured things out, he had hoped Wade wouldn't get nosy. He hoped he could control things and keep Wade safe. That was getting harder all the time. Caspian would keep his mouth shut. That much, Charlie knew, but still. He had to find a way to make Wade lose interest in those missing animals. Nothing good was at the end of that road.

"We should get some ice cream. What do you think?"

Charlie was effectively distracted by Wade's offer. In his excitement, he jumped without thinking.

Wade laughed at his enthusiasm. "That's what I thought. Let's get my truck. I'm not trying to walk to the edge of town."

Charlie picked up the pace at the idea of getting his favorite treat. Wade didn't balk at Charlie's rush to get home. He simply kept time with Charlie's stride. By the time they were in the truck and headed to Dairy Queen, Charlie couldn't sit still. He kept turning in circles and licking Wade's face and neck. At first, it was in a show of affection. Then he couldn't stop because Wade tasted too good. Plus, Wade kept laughing at his antics. Charlie loved everything about Wade. He spoiled the hell out of Charlie. Nothing made Charlie happier than when Wade smiled.

At the drive-thru window, Charlie pranced in place, impatiently waiting for his cup of vanilla ice cream topped with whipped cream. When Wade had it in hand, Charlie had to stop himself from stealing it.

As if Wade read his mind, he kept it out of Charlie's reach. "Patience, boy. Let me park and you can eat here."

Wade steered into a parking space and then set the cup in Charlie's cup holder once he was parked. Charlie lapped at the inside of the cup, doing his best not to make a mess of Wade's console and seat. Wade ran his fingers through Charlie's fur while he ate.

"Good boy. I really hate to do this to you, sweet baby. But you haven't left me much choice with the way you keep running from the vet."

Wade's words made no sense. Charlie was too distracted by his treat. Wade pinched Charlie's skin. A slight prick took Charlie by surprise. He yelped. His head spun before he could assess the damage. Charlie's gaze shot Wade's way. Wade held an empty syringe. The truck's interior moved from side to side, making Charlie dizzy. It hit him. Wade had drugged him. He couldn't maintain his magic. Charlie tried, but it was too hard with the hard-hitting sedative pumping through his system. He couldn't believe Wade would betray him like this.

Charlie's dog form fell away.

Wade's expression slackened as Charlie's body became too heavy to stay upright any longer. A strangled cry filled the truck, as if Wade tried to scream, but his throat closed on the sound.

As Charlie's body fell sideways across the console and into Wade's lap, he asked the only thing he could as the full weight of Wade's betrayal washed over him. "Why?"

The darkness took him before he got his answer.

Chapter Eleven

AFTER TEN MINUTES of sheer panic, Wade calmed down enough to drive. He couldn't move the blond head from his lap because his hands shook too hard. A small part of him was more than a little aware a nude ass was in the air for anyone he passed to see. The only explanation that felt the least bit possible was that his mind had snapped. There was no other scenario that seemed plausible. It wasn't possible there was a nude man inside his truck where Charlie should be. Wade tried not to hyperventilate as he carefully steered through town. Luckily, no one waved him down, wanting to talk. He had no clue how to defend the unconscious body in his vehicle. If anyone saw, they didn't show it. Wade prayed that meant he was the one hallucinating.

Even though Wade didn't park inside his garage often, he couldn't be seen carrying a nude guy inside his house. That meant the garage was his only option. Honestly, he didn't know where else to go but home. A thousand impossible things ran through his mind. Only one person had the answer to his questions. The man in his arms.

Wade carried Charlie through the house and dropped him on the couch. After tossing a throw blanket over him, he raced into his bedroom, where he left his duty belt, and grabbed his handcuffs. There was no way Wade could leave the guy unsecured. As he stepped back inside the living room, Charlie stirred. Wade raced across the room and quickly cuffed his hands. The meds the vet had given him shouldn't be wearing off already. Then again, they had been meant for a dog, not whatever Charlie was. If this was Charlie. Wade didn't trust his mind enough to know.

Blue eyes opened. They were the same unique blue as Charlie's eyes. Charlie glanced around. His gaze dropped to his cuffed hands and human body. Before Wade could ask a single question, Charlie was a dog again. He easily shook off the cuffs.

"What are you?"

Charlie's chin lifted. His gaze met Wade's. A low growl built in the back of his throat, sounding menacing as hell.

Wade grabbed a hardback chair from the corner and placed it bodily between them. Charlie hadn't bitten him since that first meeting, but Wade didn't feel as safe anymore.

"You drugged me."

The words rang through Wade's head. Wade's knees weakened, making him thankful for the chair to keep him upright. "Did I just hear you in my head? Why are you in my head? What are you? Are you a demon?"

Charlie's deadly stance relaxed a hair. *"Do you really think that of me? I thought I was your pet. I thought you loved me. Now you're drugging me, handcuffing me, and calling me a demon."*

"You know you won't stay at the vet. I was just trying to get you taken in without a fight to take care of your health." Wade had no idea why he was entertaining this insanity and explaining himself to a dog. But whatever was happening was his current reality, and no matter how crazy it might be, Wade had to lean into it and figure things out. That was who he was. He faced things head on.

Charlie sat and stared at him with a cocked head. *"What did you plan to do to me at the vet?"*

Wade licked his lips. "This is nuts. I've lost my mind, haven't I? My momma said my uncle Sam lost his marbles at about my age. He died in a special home. I really don't want that."

Charlie turned back into a man. He didn't move from his spot on the floor. In fact, he settled in, sitting cross-legged "You're not crazy. I'm a werewolf."

A hysterical burble of laughter rose in Wade's throat. "What about that statement is supposed to make me feel like less of a lunatic?"

Charlie looked serene, as if Wade's panic didn't bother him... or like one of them needed to remain calm and Charlie had decided it would be him. "What would make you the most comfortable? Talking to me like this? Or in the form you're used to seeing?"

Wade took a few deep breaths while he considered his options. "Well, I don't feel as crazy when I'm not hearing you in my head. But you're nude, so I don't know, really."

A smile exploded across Charlie's face, making Wade blink at the thoughts that hit with that one gesture. Charlie was beautiful, and that was wrong. So, so wrong. Wade should never, ever think that.

"I'm always naked, Wade. Since the day you brought me home, I've been nude."

That was technically true. Charlie was a dog. Dogs didn't wear clothes. Still, things were different now. "All right. I'm going to grab that throw blanket from the couch and hand it to you. No sudden moves, okay?"

Charlie rolled his eyes and stood. As he headed for the couch and grabbed the blanket for himself, Wade knew he should avert his eyes. He couldn't. Charlie looked nothing like a werewolf. Not that Wade had thought too much about what a werewolf would look like if they existed, but still. Charlie was young and unblemished in every way. He looked to be no more than twenty, and his body didn't possess an ounce of fat. He was solid yet trim muscle. Once he sat on the couch, covered by the blanket, Wade felt a little better. At least he wasn't eyeing a dog's body in a way he absolutely shouldn't be.

"I'm not a dog."

Wade's hysterics rose again. "Don't read my thoughts."

"Stop yelling them at me."

Wade took a steadying breath. He circled the chair and sat, hoping to regain some normalcy. "How old are you?"

At his question, Charlie looked taken aback, as if he expected anything but a casual conversation about ordinary things. "Nineteen."

Wade nodded. This was good. One answer meant progress toward sanity. "What's your name?"

A line appeared between Charlie's eyebrows. "Charlie."

"That's the name I gave you. What's your real name?"

"It's Charlie," Charlie said, sounding a bit irritated.

Wade let it go. "Okay. Do you have a family, Charlie?"

Charlie's open irritation deepened. "You, dumbass. Why are you asking me things you already know? You should ask what you really want to know. Yes, I was born this way. No, I don't have parents. They were killed when I was little. I was barely surviving when you found me, and no, I didn't have a name before you gave me one. Yes, I can hear your thoughts, and no, that's not because I'm psychic. We're connected because I bit you."

Wade's head spun. He wondered if he would faint. His body slumped forward, and Wade sucked air with his head between his knees. He no longer controlled what his body did. This was all too much. Werewolves weren't real. He was hallucinating, but he didn't know why. Did he have a gas leak in his house? Fuck, he didn't have gas in his house. Had Caspian cast a spell on him? He hadn't noticed, but he didn't know shit about spells. Could psychics do spells?

Charlie appeared in dog form at his side. He licked Wade's face and neck, as if trying to comfort him. Out of habit, Wade ran his fingers through Charlie's fur. Maybe the spell was wearing off and the last hour hadn't happened. He just needed some water to clear his head. Charlie had been a dog this whole time. Wade was just overheated from their walk.

"Stop freaking out. While Caspian is a powerful warlock, and he could easily make you believe all this is true, he didn't. This is real."

"Get out of my head."

At Wade's roared words, Charlie jumped away. He slunk to his dog bed at the end of the couch and plopped down. He curled up into a ball with his back to Wade. Wade didn't understand why that made him feel guilty, but it did. It wasn't in his nature to yell at Charlie. Still, the more the silence dragged on, the easier Wade breathed. Maybe he just needed to rest. Wade headed for the kitchen and drank some water. His head cleared a little more. His heartbeat slowed. It felt like he was on the right track. He would take the night off and decide what to do. Wade still thought all of this might be a dream. Everything would be better tomorrow. He would see.

THE NIGHT MOVED TOO SLOWLY for Charlie's heart. Wade refused to acknowledge him all night. Charlie didn't know what to do. A huge part of him thought maybe—if he stayed quiet and kept his head down— things would go back to normal. Maybe tomorrow, Wade would convince himself none of this was real and they would go back to being a family or whatever they had been. All Charlie knew was he loved Wade and things were different now. He felt like he couldn't breathe. If he would just go to sleep, Charlie could visit Caspian and get this settled. In the meantime, he felt like he lived in a nightmare.

Wade called in to work and made dinner. Instead of opening the usual can of dog food for Charlie, Wade made him a plate of food and left it on the kitchen floor. Charlie moved tentatively into the kitchen and ate after Wade returned to the living room. The silence dragged on, making Charlie's chest hurt. Wade normally talked to him nonstop, chattering about nothing. Tonight, there was only silence. The house was like a tomb.

After eating, Charlie lingered in the doorway between the kitchen and living room. Wade stretched out on the couch with his book. Charlie waited until Wade's mind became a steady hum, proving he had calmed down and zoned out. Then he moved back to his dog bed, hoping not to draw too much attention to himself. Wade's foot hung off the couch. Ten minutes of staring at it, and temptation beat him. Charlie licked Wade's foot. Wade smiled for half a second before it slipped away again.

"Things aren't the same."

Maybe, but Charlie had gotten a smile. He leaped onto the couch and settled into his usual spot, half on Wade's chest and half squashed against the couch. Wade's body was so tense, Charlie expected him to snap at any second. Charlie licked his neck.

"Things aren't the same," Wade repeated, between clenched teeth.

Charlie transformed into a man. "Tell me how I can make things better. I don't like you being mad at me."

Wade rolled from the couch in a flash and headed for the kitchen, leaving Charlie behind. "I need a drink."

A stuttered breath escaped Charlie. He slipped from the couch and headed for the bathroom, hoping not to cry. As he did every night, Charlie brushed his teeth before becoming a dog again. He tried avoiding his thoughts and emotions, but he was overwhelmed by the pains in his chest. After leaping onto the bed, Charlie buried his head beneath the pillow. His body shook as he sucked air, fighting the tears. It was a losing battle. Wade was all Charlie had. All he cared about. Now Wade didn't love him anymore. Wade couldn't even look at him. It hurt more than he dreamed.

The bed dipped beside him. Wade moved the pillow. Charlie turned his head, trying to hide his tears.

"This is all too weird for me. I don't know how I'm supposed to act." Wade sounded calm. That was more than Charlie expected. Still, his chest hurt and everything else too.

"How could you just stop loving me? I thought I was your best friend."

Wade released a ragged-sounding breath. "Things just aren't the same now. You're like a whole person. I can't pretend you're my pet now. People don't keep other people as pets. I just can't play like I don't know what I know."

Charlie stared at Wade, silently begging him to stop hurting him. *"You're my best friend. I love you."*

Wade shook his head. "It's not the same."

Charlie couldn't handle another word. He couldn't take another second of the rejection. His feet moved before his mind caught up with him. He had to leave. This wasn't his home any longer. It never would be again. He darted through the house, trying to run from his breaking heart. As his paws hit the grass in the backyard, Charlie sprang forward, running as fast as he could. He had to find a safe place to hunker down for the night. Then he needed to make a plan. His life in Elvenwood was over. He needed to figure out where to go next.

Chapter Twelve

Two WEEKS without Charlie had Wade a bit of a mess. People constantly asked how Charlie was doing. Wade had never noticed that before, but now he realized it had always been that way. People weren't used to seeing Wade without Charlie in tow. Wade didn't know what to tell anyone. His chest hurt all hours of the day. He couldn't stop thinking about the way Charlie had cried before running away. Wade felt like the worst person alive. He didn't have anyone to go to for advice. Each day, he felt a little more like he was coming apart at the seams. That was how he ended up three sheets to the wind at Longfellow bar. He needed to escape from himself.

Lights and sounds moved around him. Several people stopped to talk. He swore he heard Charlie's name whispered in the air. He was just a dog. Well, a wolf, and he wasn't dead. He was still out there in the world. Why did Wade feel so lost and sick? Everyone's voices seemed so much louder tonight. Wade fought the urge to cover his ears. He swore he could smell the piss-soaked bathroom and Clara's perfume from across the room. Probably because she sat near the door. Each time it opened and closed, the breeze carried the scent his way. At least, that was what Wade told himself.

"Have you met Charlie?"

Wade turned at the name. The nearest people were at a table behind him. He didn't understand why he kept hearing Charlie's name. He needed to get out of there. His skin crawled. His teeth ached. Everything hurt. The alcohol made everything worse and churned in his gut. He stumbled from his stool. Wade focused on putting one foot in front of the other, trying to make it to the door. He didn't know where he was headed, but he needed to go.

"I'm thinking about asking Charlie on a date."

Wade stumbled at the words. He didn't know if he heard right. Wade still thought his mind played tricks on him, but his gaze moved Clara's way, nonetheless. He blatantly eavesdropped.

"I know he's blond and I know Caspian said my soulmate has dark hair. But really, I'm starting to question Caspian's vision. I've spoken with all the dark-haired men in town."

Rage and some form of irritated fuck it rose inside Wade as he stared at the blonde he had known his whole life. He didn't know if he truly overheard Clara's whispered conversation or if his imagination played tricks on him, but he couldn't stop himself from butting in.

Wade sliced his hand through the air in Clara's direction. "For fuck's sake, Clara. Get a goddamn clue. It's Scott. I know it's Scott. Your mom knows it's Scott. Damn, the guy who cuts my hair three towns over probably knows it's Scott. You're the only person who's too damn blind to see the way he looks at you. Fuck," he added with a growl as he shoved his way outside. Clara's slack-jawed expression might have made him laugh if he wasn't in so much pain.

Everything sucked. Why should Clara be immune to the suckage?

The night air didn't help clear his mind or dampen his fury. The full moon seemed too bright. A nearby streetlamp buzzed so loud, he wondered if he might go deaf. He moved toward the tree line next to the bar. Cutting through the woods seemed like a safer option. At this point, he might accidentally, on purpose, stumble out into oncoming traffic to stop the feelings he didn't want. There was something ugly growing inside him. Thoughts he couldn't let intrude beat at his brain. Haunting dreams he didn't dare acknowledge grew larger every day. Wade felt like he raced toward a horrible realization, and he didn't know how to stop. He should have grabbed a beer for the road. Hopefully, he had some liquor left at home. Wade needed to drown this out.

Crickets, frogs, and something else in the distance assaulted his eardrums. Wade covered his ears and kept moving. Each step he took, his feet got heavier. His visioned darkened. The sound of a thousand heartbeats drowned out his ragged breathing. He closed his eyes, and everything disappeared.

A FLY BUZZED HIS EAR. Wade swatted blindly. The scent of blood assaulted Wade's senses, immediately clearing his head. His eyes snapped open. Light pierced his skull, making his stomach churn and pulling his eyes closed again. A metallic taste lingered on his tongue. Wade licked his lips and tried harder to open his eyes. He peeked one eye open and immediately scrambled away at the sight of bloody chunks next to him. His gaze shot around the room. He was home. In his living room. The sun shone bright through the windows and Wade had no idea how he came to be there. He forced his gaze toward the pile of flesh, fur, and organs in the center of the floor. His stomach heaved before he could decipher what he looked at. Wade rushed to the bathroom. He barely made it to the commode before the contents of his stomach came flying out. Wade puked until there was nothing left. Then he dry heaved until his lungs nearly quit. For several minutes, he stayed on the bathroom floor, praying for death. Everything hurt and felt too sensitive to the touch. Reality didn't feel very real any longer. He forced himself to look at his hands. They were covered in dried blood. He pushed to his knees. The room spun. He clung to the toilet while he caught his breath. When the room steadied, he moved to his feet. He caught sight of his reflection and froze. Leaves and twigs stuck to his hair. His face was covered in blood. He started the shower, hoping to cling to the tiniest hint of reality.

Wade knew he should go back to the living room and assess what he had done. He couldn't. Not yet. His brain still shied away from the truth. In some small way, Wade recognized he was in shock. His brain was too big of a mess to deal. As he stepped beneath the hot water, his teeth chattered. Tears pressed at the backs of his eyes. No matter how hot he made the water, his skin felt like ice. He couldn't remember a thing. The last thing he recalled was cutting through the woods to his house. His vision had blurred and then nothing. The entire night was just gone.

He looked down; dirty water swirled around his feet as the blood washed from his body. A vision or a memory flared to life in his head. He couldn't tell which. *The human version of Charlie climbed into the shower with him and washed his skin.* Wade rubbed his eyes. It wasn't real. He squeezed his eyes shut and dipped his head beneath the water. The image in his mind turned clearer by the second.

Charlie kissed his neck and chest. Wade grabbed his throat and claimed his mouth, taking control.

Wade shook his head. It wasn't possible. That never happened. What was wrong with him? Maybe he really had lost his mind. He had to know what he had done. Wade needed to focus on that. He scrubbed his hair and skin until all evidence of blood disappeared, clinging to what he could control. Once he was clean, he quickly dressed and brushed his teeth until he felt certain he lost a coat of enamel, but the flavor of blood disappeared. Wade took a deep breath for courage and returned to the living room. He forced himself to approach the mess like an investigator rather than a madman. From what he could decipher, it was three squirrels, a groundhog, and a beaver. It looked as if their necks had been broken and bites had been taken of them—like they had been used as chew toys by a rabid dog. The mess didn't belong to a human. At least, that was something. Animals were one thing. He couldn't handle a dead person in his living room. Wade locked down his mind and grabbed the cleaning supplies. He refused to let himself think as he tossed the bodies into a garbage bag. Once the house was clean, he headed for the backyard. He needed to bury the bag. Otherwise, the carcasses might attract wildlife. He grabbed a shovel and started digging in a spot where it looked like Charlie had already been rearranging the dirt. Three feet in, something shiny caught his eye. Wade gingerly pushed the soil around with the tip of his shovel, scraping around the sparkling object to get a better look.

As realization sank in, his ass hit the ground. Wade stared into the hole. It was Hank's cat, Princess. There wasn't much left of her, but he recognized the collar. Tears blurred Wade's vision. What was happening to his life? He didn't understand. He sucked a deep breath, trying to control the panic. Nothing helped. The pains in his chest felt like knives in his heart. He closed his eyes and fought for calm. Everything was a mess. Another memory over-whelmed him.

"Come on, baby. I've got it. You couldn't help it. It's my fault for biting you. Just go inside and let me take care of everything."

"I didn't mean to hurt Princess. Hank will be so brokenhearted."

Charlie kissed the corner of his mouth. "Don't cry. It's not your fault. I'll bury her. No one has to know. You should drink the stuff Caspian made for you. By tomorrow, you won't remember any of this. Just let me help."

Wade took a breath. *Caspian.* He shot to his feet and tossed the trash bag in the hole before quickly shoveling dirt over it. He had to see Caspian. With the animals buried, he grabbed his keys and jumped into his truck. He didn't think. Wade just drove. Since Caspian only lived two streets over, Wade was there in no time. He leaped from the truck and headed for the door like his ass was on fire. It wasn't until his knuckles skimmed the door that he realized he didn't know what to say. There was no way to start this conversation.

The door opened, so did Wade's mouth. Nothing came out. Tears blurred his vision.

Caspian's sweet brown eyes flashed with understanding. "Come inside. You could use some coffee."

Wade followed on Caspian's heels on autopilot. Caspian motioned toward the couch and Wade sat.

He stared at nothing, seeing nothing, as he waited for Caspian to hand him a cup of coffee. He rocked himself in full-on meltdown mode. When he finally took the first sip of Caspian's coffee, calm settled over him. The tightness in his chest eased.

Caspian smiled. "Better?"

Wade nodded.

"Keep drinking."

The way Caspian urged him to drink made Wade wonder if there was something in the cup other than coffee, but at this point, he couldn't care. Life was already in shambles. He took another sip. He felt better by the second.

"What's happening to me?"

"You have lycanthropy sickness," Caspian said without an ounce of mercy.

Wade blinked. "What?"

Caspian flashed him an understanding smile. "When Charlie bit you, he gave you lycanthropy sickness. You're human, so you can't fully become a werewolf, but you are affected by the full moon. It turns you a bit... wild."

He didn't know where to begin. "How long have you known?"

"Since the first full moon after Charlie bit you. He came to me, hoping I could cure you, but there's no cure. No magic can fix this. Instead, he asked me to help you deal with the aftereffects. Apparently, you didn't take the news well. So I made him a potion to help you forget. In return, he keeps you from hurting people while you're stuck in the frenzy."

Wade wanted to cover his ears and call Caspian a liar. But he knew in his heart it was true and the flashes of memories felt too real. Plus, there was no pretending this morning hadn't happened.

"I killed Princess."

Caspian's expression turned sympathetic. "I know."

Wade's irritation spiked. "You said you'd help me if I brought you something belonging to one of the missing animals. What did you plan to do when I showed up with Princess's collar in hand?"

Caspian shrugged. "I figured I'd just tell you I didn't see anything."

Wade's eyes fell closed. He scrubbed his forehead. "I don't know what's real anymore." Charlie had been helping him. Wade had been so cruel to him. There was no taking it back.

"I'm sorry."

Wade's eyes shot open at the sound of Charlie's voice.

Charlie hovered in the mouth of the hallway, looking unsure of his welcome. In jeans and a t-shirt, he appeared more human than ever. Wade's heart tried to do a somersault at the sight of him.

Charlie rubbed his arm, looking nervous and ready to bolt. "I tried to fix you and then I tried to help." His eyes filled with tears, shattering Wade's heart. "I never meant to do anything bad to you."

An invisible weight sat on Wade's chest. "I know."

Caspian stood. "I'll leave you two alone." He squeezed Charlie's shoulder as he passed, heading down the hall.

Once they were alone, Charlie moved deeper into the room. He still looked like he might bolt any second. His beautiful blue gaze stayed locked on Wade, as if he couldn't look anywhere else.

Wade set his coffee aside and cleared his throat. "Is this where you've been?"

Charlie nodded. "I didn't know where else to go."

"You could've come home."

Pain filled Charlie's expression at Wade's claim. "We both know that's not true."

Wade cleared his throat again. Even to his ears, he sounded uncomfortable, but he was happier to see Charlie than he could express. He had to keep talking. "I remembered something. At least, I think I did." He couldn't force himself to confess his memories. "I don't know what's real."

Charlie shuffled a little closer. "What did you remember?"

His eyes were so fucking hypnotic. Wade couldn't look away. He licked his lips. Wade didn't know if he could say the words. He couldn't stop seeing Charlie kissing his throat and chest, moving lower.

Charlie's eyes shimmered, almost becoming luminescent.

"I don't know what's real," Wade repeated.

"Yes, you do."

Wade's breathing quickened. The images in his mind became clearer by the second. Charlie wasn't his pet. He had been there, taking care of Wade. Saving him from himself. Loving him. Selflessly keeping sentry. Taking away the memories that hurt, even though that meant hurting himself. Wade remembered everything.

"You left me."

Hurt like Wade had never seen flashed in Charlie's eyes. "You didn't want me anymore."

"I could never not want you."

Charlie drew a ragged-sounding breath at Wade's confession. "I ruined your life."

Wade shook his head. "You gave me a reason to live."

"I made you forget me."

Pain sliced through Wade's chest. "Yeah. I am a little mad about that."

A smile exploded across Charlie's face. It disappeared as quickly as it came. "I would give anything if you could've met me in this form. If I had never bitten you, and we'd met at the corner store, then maybe you wouldn't be ashamed. Maybe you would've loved me."

"I do love you." Life was a huge fucking mess. Wade had a lot to work through. He had a problem he didn't know how to fix or control, but he remembered the way Charlie had cared for him. He remembered the heated nights they had shared when he had been in the throes of his first frenzied full moons. Wade had craved the hunt. His skin had itched to kill. Charlie had been there, giving him a different focus. He had done whatever it had taken to keep Wade sane. Even when that meant taking away the memories of them. Even when it meant stealing the memory of their love.

Wade stood.

Charlie took a step back.

Wade lost his breath at the move. "Why are you afraid of me?"

Charlie swallowed.

"You two should kiss and make up. Not that I'm a voyeur or anything." Caspian didn't look the least bit guilty for spying on them from around the corner.

Wade raised his eyebrows at Charlie, silently begging him to make the next move.

Charlie closed the space between them and walked into Wade's waiting arms.

Wade pressed his lips to the top of Charlie's head and breathed in his scent. "Please come home. I need you."

Charlie nodded.

"Awwww," Caspian cooed from the hallway.

The pains in Wade's chest eased. He still had a lot to figure out, but he had Charlie back in his life. Funny how that one detail made everything else seem bearable. Wade wouldn't lose him again. That was a promise.

THE RIDE HOME was made in silence, but Wade held his hand. That meant everything to Charlie. Charlie fought back tears on the short drive. He had been so torn this past year with Wade. On one hand, Charlie wanted the intimacy Wade always craved during the full moon. On the other, Charlie never meant to doom Wade to this life of feral moonbeams. If giving up Wade meant he could take back the nightmare life he had cursed Wade to live, he would. In a heartbeat, he would. Charlie loved him. He wanted Wade to be happy.

"I wish there had been a way for Caspian to take away the memories of my sickness without stealing you."

Wade's sudden confession brought a sad smile to Charlie's lips. "Me too, but there was no way to separate knowing about your illness and learning about me. Until you saw me, and you know how that went."

It was different when Wade lost his humanity to the sickness. Wade recognized his mate in those moments, no matter how many times Caspian scrubbed Charlie from his mind. For the rest of the month, Wade was oblivious to him. The past year had been the hardest of Charlie's life, and that was saying a lot for an orphan whose parents had been viciously murdered when he was two.

Wade put the truck in park in the driveway and turned slightly to stare at Charlie. Silence grew between them. Wade visibly swallowed. Charlie felt Wade's hurt and the fear slowly returning. He was across the cab in an instant. Charlie couldn't let Wade's mind go back to a bad place. Wade didn't fight him as their lips met.

"It's okay," Charlie whispered against his lips. "I'll take care of you."

Wade buried his fingers in Charlie's hair and held him in place as he explored Charlie's mouth. Charlie let his hands roam. He stroked Wade's stomach and chest, needing to touch Wade everywhere. No one could know how much he missed Wade. Every day without him had been hell. It tore at his soul to think about living without him.

"Stop," Wade begged while still trying to taste Charlie's lips. "I can feel you hurting. I hate it."

"You said things aren't the same." As happy as Charlie was to have Wade accepting him, he couldn't forget those words. They had cut him to the bone when Charlie had needed Wade's love the most.

Wade cupped Charlie's face and held him away. His gaze moved over Charlie's features, as if searching for something only he understood. He opened his mouth, looking like a man bent on baring his soul. A knock landed on the window, pulling their attention that way. Clara stood outside, chewing her bottom lip.

Wade turned the key far enough to roll down the window.

Clara's gaze moved Charlie's way for a half a second. "Hey, Charlie." She focused on Wade again before he had time to respond. "Hey, Wade. Can I talk to you for a second?"

With a nod, Wade rolled up the window and handed the keys to Charlie. "You go on inside. I'll be there in a minute."

Charlie slipped from the truck and headed for the door without looking back. With his heightened senses, he still heard every word.

"I saw you pull up," Clara said, as if that explained her presence.

"Okay." Wade sounded confused and more than a little wary.

Clara took a deep breath, as if trying to calm her nerves. Charlie heard the anxiousness in her voice. "I just wanted to say I'm sorry about last night. When I said that shit about asking Charlie on a date, I didn't realize you were standing there, but I also didn't know you two were dating. Now that I know, I don't blame you for jumping down my throat. I would've done the same thing in your shoes."

Charlie lingered behind the closed front door—frozen in fascination as he listened to their conversation.

"No. Please," Wade said, sounding slightly embarrassed. "Don't worry about it. I'm the one who's sorry. Charlie and I had a bit of an argument, and I had too much to drink. You didn't deserve to have me attacking you last night."

He heard Clara shift from foot to foot. When she spoke again, he could hear the smile in her voice. "It's really cute that you ended up dating someone named Charlie. Just like your dog. Where is he anyhow? I haven't seen him around in a while."

"He's in the house." Charlie smiled. It wasn't a lie. Wade kept laying it on, though. "Caspian says there's a cosmic reason I named my dog Charlie—like I subconsciously knew that was my soulmate's name."

"Awwww."

Charlie covered his mouth, fighting a laugh at Clara's loud exclamation of joy. Clara was such a sucker for Caspian's predictions, and Wade knew it. Wade was an amazing person. He knew exactly how to make other people feel like their oddities weren't odd at all —just like Clara's penchant for believing in fortune-telling.

"Well, I'll let you get back to the two Charlies then. I just saw you pull up and couldn't let the chance slip me by to make things right. We've been neighbors and friends for a long time. I don't want anything to change."

"Me either."

Charlie moved to the couch and sat as their conversation came to a close.

Wade came through the door, looking sexy as hell. Charlie could tell he hadn't bothered brushing his hair this morning. The brown locks stood in every direction. A shadow of hair covered his jaw from not shaving. His wide shoulders always took up too much space. Charlie loved everything about him, especially the way his dark green gaze always found Charlie in the room before looking anywhere else. He had to take a breath as it happened now.

"So how exactly does Clara know you?"

A smile snapped to Charlie's lips. "After Caspian took me in, I started going to work with him every day. He introduced me around town as his cousin from New Orleans. Caspian said you'd come for me soon, and everyone would need to adjust to seeing the human side of me." Charlie shrugged. "I didn't really think you'd want me back, but I still did what he said."

Wade crossed the room and dropped to his knees at Charlie's feet. He wrapped his arms around Charlie's waist and hauled him to the edge of the couch. His gaze bored into Charlie's, leaving no doubt whatever he said next was important.

"I'm sorry."

Charlie swallowed hard at Wade's intensity.

Wade didn't let up. "From the bottom of my heart, I'm so fucking sorry. You've been taking care of me for a year, and I failed you when you needed me."

Charlie stroked Wade's cheek. "I love you. There's nothing I wouldn't do to make you happy, even if it means you have to forget me."

Wade shook his head. "That's not an acceptable option for me. You should've forced me to deal with this illness sooner."

A sad smile tugged at Charlie's lips. "You must not recall how badly you've taken each full moon. I couldn't watch you hate yourself." Charlie took a ragged breath. "I couldn't watch you grow to hate me."

Wade shrugged. "I don't think that's possible. You're the best part of me."

"You're getting better. You controlled yourself last night without my help. You only gnawed on some wildlife."

A smile exploded across Wade's face as Charlie projected his thoughts at Wade. "You're in my head. How could I possibly live without you?"

"Is it bad if I say I hope you can't?"

Wade's smile slipped away. He held tightly to Charlie's waist and stood. "You're mine. I'm never letting you go." He claimed Charlie's mouth as he blindly headed for the bedroom. Not all the ferocity from the full moon had left Wade yet. Charlie felt the neediness inside him. He had run wild through the woods and hunted. Now Wade needed his mate. Charlie would give him everything.

The moment Wade tossed Charlie onto the bed, Charlie scrambled out of the clothes he hated. It went against his nature to cover his body, but he recognized he had to fit in. If he hoped to have a real life with Wade, he needed to act normal. But in this space, he was free, and Wade needed him.

Wade ripped away his clothes too, as if he couldn't get rid of them fast enough. When their nude bodies came together again, Charlie nearly howled in relief. This was the other half of him. Charlie felt lost without him.

Even though Wade managed to get Charlie lubed—barely, and between heated kisses—the way Wade impaled him was almost violent. They tore at each other's skin, biting and clawing, while trying to get closer. The wounds healed as fast as they appeared. With his teeth sunk into Charlie's shoulder, Wade thrust over and over again, taking Charlie in a way that could only be a claiming. Charlie held on and savored every second. His entire being stayed hyper focused on every sensation. The friction between them massaged Charlie's cock while Wade pounded at the perfect angle. Tension built until Charlie thought his head might explode. When his orgasm finally hit, a roar ripped from his throat, sounding almost deadly. Wade cried out against Charlie's skin, pumping him full of cum. In that moment, all was right with the world. Wade remembered everything. Charlie would hold his hand and walk with him through the new life he had been given. Everything would be fine. Not only did Charlie feel that in his spirit, but Caspian had also promised it was true.

Charlie believed. In Wade's arms, everything felt possible.

Chapter Thirteen

WADE PACED THE FLOOR. It had been a trying day and his brain felt like it was on fire. Sounds were too loud. His living room felt oppressive. Guilt had finally driven him to return Princess's collar to Hank. He had spared Hank the details but admitted Princess was gone. He swore to himself he would find a way to make things right with everyone in town who had been affected by his illness, even though no one but Caspian knew. Everything just felt heavier than normal today.

Charlie trotted into the room. He transformed from wolf to man. His collar caught the sunlight and glimmered. Pride rose in Wade's chest. There was a time when everything about them would have felt wrong to Wade. Those days were long gone. Charlie was the greatest love of Wade's life. He wouldn't survive without him. According to Caspian, their kind lived very long lives. Long enough people would eventually become suspicious. It made him a little sad to think he would eventually have to move away from this town. But Charlie would always be at his side, and that was all that mattered.

Wade forced himself to move to the couch and sit. Pacing wasn't helping the growing tension inside him.

"There's a full moon tonight."

Wade nodded at Charlie's words. He knew that, and he had been a bit of a mess over it all day. That, on top of his visit with Hank, had him ready to crawl from his skin. It was the first full moon since Caspian stopped taking his memories. He was nervous as hell. Wade didn't want to hurt anyone or anything. But he could feel the night coming and his skin itched a little more with each passing second.

Charlie moved to the couch and straddled Wade's lap. "Don't worry. I won't let you do anything bad."

"I don't want to hurt any more animals. That's not me."

Charlie nodded. "I know, and I've been thinking about that. Instead of steering you toward hunting animals to keep the townsfolk safe, I had a different idea for tonight."

Wade's eyebrows rose. He couldn't hide his skepticism. "You're not planning to set me loose in the meat section of Piggly Wiggly, are you?"

The way Charlie laughed eased the tightness in Wade's chest. It also didn't hurt that Charlie was nude in his lap. That made a lot of things easier to endure. "No." He held up a pair of handcuffs Charlie hadn't seen him holding. "I thought maybe I'd chain you to the bed instead."

A feral part of Wade howled to life at the idea of being chained. The human part of him was all in. "How will you keep me entertained? I'd hate to tear our bed to pieces, trying to get free."

Charlie's eyelids lowered. His expression turned seductive. "I have my ways."

Wade wrapped his arms around Charlie and shot to his feet. He headed to the bedroom without a second thought. "We'd better get started then. I can feel the sun setting."

A sexy smile played on Charlie's lips, giving Wade more confidence than anything ever had. His life was different now. One night a month, he was a little out of control. Charlie looked like he had the cure for that, and Wade couldn't wait to test this new plan. What was one night a month, really? Especially since he had gained the entire world in exchange. Wade wouldn't change a thing about his life now. It was perfect.

Introduction to Witchin Wildcat

In the small town of Elvenwood, everyone knows everyone else. That makes it hard to meet new people. It's a good thing they're being overrun by a new population: supernatural creatures.

Hank has owned Elvenwood Liquors since his dad passed five years ago, leaving him in charge. His life is pretty quiet. He works and keeps to himself. In a town where everyone is a little strange, people still find him odd. That's because he knows all of Elvenwood's secrets. It's only a matter of time before no one can escape the truth. There's a reason certain beings are attracted to Elvenwood, and not everything headed their way has good intentions. It's

Hank's self-appointed job to sort the good from the bad. That's a job that gets a little harder each day, especially since the next creature coming to town is meant for him.

Witchin Wildcat is the fourth book in Charity Parkerson's Witchin series. These fun, short paranormal romances are meant to be devoured on your lunch break. Read along as a tiny town in Ohio grows its supernatural community one resident at a time.

Chapter Fourteen

EACH NIGHT, Hank closed his liquor store at exactly seven. He didn't doubt he lost some business to bigger counties because of the early closing. Hank couldn't care. He already worked six days a week. Hell would freeze before he put any more pressure on himself than he already faced. Being a workaholic had been all his father had known. It had driven him into an early grave. Hank had no plans to be that guy. Life was stressful enough in a town like Elvenwood. In fact, if he didn't live so close to work, he would close earlier. He didn't like people enough to care if they had time to get their wine after work. They could grab a six-pack from the Gas and Zoom two blocks over for all he cared. So Hank couldn't explain why it was ten after seven and he hadn't locked the doors yet. Mostly, it was because he was fascinated.

For twenty minutes, Hank's gaze followed his last customer of the night. The guy was too young to buy alcohol. That much Hank didn't doubt. He told himself he relished the challenge. Hank loved to put underage buyers in their place. That didn't explain the way his eyes kept eating the man alive. Hell, it was possible the blond beauty was twenty-one, but he definitely wasn't a day older. His olive skin and dark brown eyes didn't match his hair color, yet Hank knew it wasn't dyed, because Hank also knew something else. The guy wasn't human.

Hank had grown up in Elvenwood. He had spent his entire life in the woods surrounding the city. In fact, he had to leave each night out the back door to cut through the woods to get to his cabin. His whole life, he had seen past the faces people presented to the world, to the magic they hid below. Hank's mom was Fae. She had given birth to Hank and then left him on his father's doorstep. While his dad had hidden nothing from Hank, Hank wasn't sure that had entirely been a good thing. It might have been better to let Hank think he was crazy. Instead, the entire town thought he was. He spoke to creatures they couldn't see. Where magic existed, Hank saw its crackling light, even if he couldn't decipher exactly what power a person held. As a child, he hadn't known he should keep those thoughts and knowledge to himself. Hank knew now. Everyone thought he had mental issues.

His late-night customer finally found his way to the register. With one hip leaned against the counter and his arms crossed over his chest, Hank waited. His heart beat a little faster with each step the man made in his direction. Hank swore the guy moved with a sleek grace he had never seen before. He had a familiar scent, but Hank couldn't place it. It was as if he cast a spell over Hank. In that moment, he understood how his father had been easily seduced by his mother. Magic had an allure that had cost many men their lives since the beginning of time. Hank could see himself giving this man everything.

The guy set a single rum-infused cocktail container on the counter.

Hank fought a snort. "It took you twenty minutes to pick out one drink?"

A sexy smirk pulled at the man's lips. "Honestly, I was waiting to see if you would lose patience with me and toss me out. You disappointed me. I was looking forward to having your hands all over me. This drink looked like the most disgusting you sell. So I decided to make dissatisfaction my theme for the night."

Hank fought a smile. At least the guy was fun. "ID."

The man's smile grew. "I guess you've decided to be let down tonight too." He passed Hank an ID. "I'm most certainly *a day* older than twenty-one."

Hank tried hiding his surprise. Whatever the man was, he could read minds. Hank hadn't seen that one coming. He inspected the license. "Tafari Zhang. Twenty-two. Yes. How dare I think you're young." Hank didn't bother keeping the snideness from his tone as he handed back the ID. He didn't even remember being twenty-two. Thirty-eight was fucking ancient by comparison.

"Mhmm. Yes. Everyone knows thirty-eight is the new ninety, especially since you can't die."

Hank wasn't as good at hiding his surprise this time. "What are you?"

Tafari's eyes flashed amber before turning brown again. It could have been a trick of the light, but Hank wasn't dumb. "I don't know what you mean."

Hank held the plastic bottle of cocktail out to Tafari. "Free of charge, if you show me your true face."

Tafari took a step back and shoved his hands in his pockets. "Maybe next time." He winked before walking away. Hank watched his every step until he disappeared from sight. With a shake of his head, he moved to lock the door. Even then, Hank found himself looking right and left, searching the street for any sign of his visitor.

"This town is getting damn strange."

Hank glanced behind him at Relic's claim. The sprite who lived in his cellar sat perched on the counter. "That it is."

Hank set the alarm and turned out the lights.

"Goodnight, Hank."

"See you tomorrow, Relic," he said on the way to back the door. Maybe he would see Tafari tomorrow night, too. It was a nice thought. Hank hadn't had anything to look forward to in a long time. He would take what he could get, especially a sexy stranger.

TAFARI WATCHED Hank lock the back door of his liquor store and step into the woods. He kept to the trees, silently following the way he did every night. Elvenwood wasn't as safe as it used to be. The Elven spells surrounding the town that kept evil at bay weakened each day. Already Caspian and Brock had been forced to kill a couple of zombies. There were vulnerabilities in the town's defenses. Hank couldn't keep pretending to be normal. He needed to embrace his magic. Otherwise, they would soon be overrun by darkness. Tafari didn't mind the few peaceful creatures that had found their way here over the years. Even though they could slightly be reckless with their powers, and people's cats ended up dead. Tafari still believed the new additions were good. But it was only a matter of time before a bad one came along and Elvenwood needed all the magic they could get.

"I know your scent now. How long have you been following me?"

Tafari's laughter sounded like a deep purr. He stuck to the shadows, staying hidden from sight.

"Tonight? Or in general?"

"Oh. You're in my head. The plot thickens."

"Maybe you're in mine."

Hank circled the tree where Tafari hid, but he didn't look up. Tafari pressed against the tree's trunk, staying out of sight while he listened to Hank's voice moving below him. "I don't read minds. That's not my parlor trick."

"What is your trick, then? Show me."

"I thought you could read minds." Hank stopped moving.

"No. I hear your thoughts. That's not the same."

Tafari peered around the thick limb where he was perched. Hank was gone. Disappointment washed over him. It had been a long time since anyone spoke to him.

"Oh. You're an Asian leopard cat."

Hank's sudden appearance at Tafari's side sent him scrambling. He lost his balance. His life flashed before his eyes as he clawed the air, trying for purchase. Then he was fine. He was in Hank's strong arms and firmly on the ground. Hank inspected him up close, as if Tafari wouldn't scratch his eyes out. He wouldn't, but still.

"Beautiful," Hank murmured before setting Tafari on the ground. Tafari might have blushed had he been in his human form. "I thought cats were graceful."

Tafari hissed at the insult. *"You're the one who scared me."*

A sexy smirk touched Hank's lips. "You're the one who started it."

That was fair. Still, rude. Tafari twitched his tail in his irritation.

Hank stepped over him. "Well, come on, then."

Tafari cautiously followed in Hank's tracks. *"Where are we going?"*

"I owe you a drink."

"I don't actually drink alcohol. It's not good for me."

Hank flashed a smile over his shoulder. He was like a sexy lumberjack. Dark hair and blue eyes. Tafari was transfixed. "I'm sure I can find something you'll like. We made a deal. I don't break my word."

Since it seemed to be important to Hank and Tafari kind of liked the idea of spending more time in Hank's company, he let Hank lead the way. As they reached Hank's cabin, curiosity got the best of Tafari.

"Why are you being so kind to me when you're so grumpy with all the people you've known your whole life?"

"I like animals better than people. People suck."

Hank stuck his keys in the door.

Tafari shifted into his human form and spoke close to Hank's ear. "I can be a person too."

Hank turned. Only inches separated their bodies. His gaze stayed locked on Tafari's face, as if he forced himself not to eye Tafari's nudity. He unbuttoned his flannel shirt. "It's only in looks. We both know you're more animal at heart." Hank shrugged off his shirt and tossed it over Tafari's shoulders.

Tafari automatically slid his arms inside the sleeves. The material was still warm from Hank's skin. It smelled like him. A deep contented purr vibrated in the back of Tafari's throat.

"I like that sound."

Hank fascinated Tafari. He couldn't tear his gaze from Hank's hard lines. Hank looked angry—like he might lash out at the world at any moment, but he was gentle with Tafari. "Does my nudity make you uncomfortable?"

A slight smile touched Hank's lips. "Not uncomfortable, no." He turned away and opened the door. Tafari stroked the shirt. It was soft and swallowed him whole. The sleeves had been rolled up to Hank's elbows. On Tafari, those same rolled-up sleeves fell to his wrists.

Cool air and the scent of apples washed over Tafari as he stepped inside the cabin. The lights flared to life, showing off a manly home. Everything was made of real wood and looked sturdy. As a Fae, Hank would be more connected to the earth. Tafari imagined he had a strong belief in natural materials. But Tafari wasn't here to inspect the furniture. He was here for Hank.

The living room and kitchen seemed to be one huge, interconnected room with only an island and furniture separating the space. Hank dumped his keys on the island and headed for the fridge. "Are you hungry?"

Tafari's ears perked. It had been a while since he last ate.

Hank glanced over his shoulder. "You're hungry. Do you like chicken?"

Tafari moved a little closer. He liked chicken.

A soft chuckle rumbled from Hank's chest, warming Tafari's skin. "He likes chicken," Hank said, as if speaking to himself.

To hide his smile and enjoy Hank's scent, Tafari buried his nose inside the borrowed shirt. Hank turned with a plate of cold chicken in hand, catching him. As Hank had said, Tafari was an animal at heart. Scent was important. He refused to be ashamed. The food caught his attention. Tafari moved to the island and easily climbed on top. He eyed the plate. It smelled like roasted chicken and looked to have already been deboned. Hank held up a piece and Tafari ate it from between Hank's fingers.

Flavor exploded on his tongue. "Delicious."

Hank smiled. "Would you like me to heat it up?"

Tafari shook his head. "This is fine."

Hank fed him another piece.

Tafari relished being served.

"How does some milk sound?"

"Yum. Milk."

Hank turned away and grabbed a glass from the cabinet. Tafari stole another bite while Hank poured him a glass of milk. "You're welcome to eat as much as you want. I've already had dinner."

Tafari shoved another bite in his mouth and chewed. Living in the wild meant freedom, but meals were sometimes scarce.

Hank handed him the milk. He watched while Tafari drank. Tafari felt the calm hum of Hank's mind, as if he purposefully hid his thoughts from Tafari.

"Most humans don't sit on the counter."

Tafari flashed him a feral smile. "I'm not human." He immediately felt guilty despite his words. Hank had fed him. "But I can move to a chair if it would make you more comfortable."

Hank shook his head. "I don't care. I was just pointing out the obvious."

Maybe, but Tafari still moved from the island to a nearby barstool. He dragged the plate closer and ate while Hank supervised.

"How do you know so much about me? Earlier, you said I can't die. That wasn't a thought I was having."

Tafari sipped his milk before answering. "Tonight wasn't the first time we've met. We met when I was only a few weeks old. I had been tossed from a car window. You fixed my broken paw." He held up his left hand.

A smile exploded across Hank's features. "That was you? Damn. That was so long ago, I forgot all about it."

A hint of sadness washed over Tafari. He was so forgettable while Tafari remembered everything about that day. Hank had been kind. He had used magic to heal Tafari while whispering praise and stroking him. Hank was burned into his memories while Tafari had disappeared from Hank's mind.

Tafari slipped from the stool. "Thank you for the food and milk. I'll leave your shirt outside."

A line appeared between Hank's eyebrows. "What did I say wrong?"

Tafari kept his gaze averted. "It's nothing. I should go."

Hank was across the room in an instant. He stroked Tafari from the top of his head to the small of his back.

Tafari's nerves settled.

Hank did it again. "It's okay. You don't have to go. It's supposed to get pretty chilly tonight. You should stay here with me where it's warm."

Tafari eyed Hank's expression. He truly wanted Tafari to stay. With a nod, Tafari sealed Hank's fate. Hank just didn't know it yet.

Chapter Fifteen

HANK HAD ALWAYS preferred animals to people. They were less complicated and didn't think he was crazy when he spoke to beings they couldn't see. Of course, most animals could see the sprites that lived all over Elvenwood. People, on the other hand, were not for him.

Tafari didn't feel like an animal. Even curled up in a ball in cat form next to him on the couch, Hank knew Tafari could become a man. A beautiful man. Fucking breathtaking, really. He couldn't force himself to leave Tafari's side until he knew Tafari slept peacefully. Tafari had tried to leave him earlier. Hank didn't understand why that bothered him so much, but it did. He couldn't let Tafari head back out into the cold. He belonged here with Hank.

Hank headed to the bathroom with his mind churning. Throughout his shower and brushing his teeth, Hank mused over Tafari's reaction right before he tried to leave. He turned their conversation over in his mind, searching for what set him off. The only thing that made sense was that Hank had forgotten him. That obviously mattered to Tafari. It wasn't that Hank had forgotten him as much as it had been nearly twenty-two years ago. He had been sixteen at the time, and once Tafari's paw had been healed, he had disappeared into the woods. Hank had wanted to go after him, but his father had been adamant Hank couldn't have any more pets. Between Hank's penchant for bringing creatures home and his father's allergies, his dad had been completely fed up with Hank. He had put that day out of his mind. It seemed Tafari hadn't and that hurt Hank's chest for reasons he didn't understand.

With his nightly routine out of the way, Hank headed to bed. As he crawled beneath the covers, Tafari leaped onto his chest and then made his way underneath the blanket. As he curled against Hank's side, he became human once more. With his head on

Hank's chest, Tafari snaked an arm and leg across Hank's body.

Hank stared at the ceiling and tried not to think. They were nude. Tafari kept rubbing his head on Hank's chest like a cat. A slight purr hummed from Tafari's chest, vibrating against Hank's skin. He didn't know how to act or where to put his hands. Everything felt completely out of his element. Then Tafari started licking his chest—like he was cleaning Hank. Hank's cock stirred. It was out of his control. His mind was all over the place. He kept his hands to himself and tried to clear his mind.

Tafari shifted positions, straddling Hank's body. He licked Hank's neck and chin. When he licked Hank's lips, a ragged breath escaped Hank. Tafari's tongue slipped inside Hank's mouth. Hank let it happen. Tafari explored Hank's mouth while Hank burned and fought against himself. He wasn't an active participant, but neither did he fight.

Before Hank knew it would happen, Tafari sat back on his dick. As Hank's cock sank into an already lubed hole, he realized he had been seduced. Tafari had planned this. Even with that truth invading his mind, Hank didn't know what to do. They didn't feel wrong, but the human side of his brain wondered if they should. Then Tafari lifted and sat again, rocking himself on Hank's dick and taking what he wanted. Hank gripped the sheets. He fought the urge to pump inside Tafari's tight ass. Instead, he left everything to Tafari. For sanity's sake, he needed that buffer. Hank needed to be able to tell himself Tafari had fucked him when this night was over. He hadn't taken Tafari.

No matter who was in charge, Hank's balls drew up tight. His heels dug into the mattress as he moved closer to the edge. Tafari bounced on Hank's cock, making sounds Hank had never heard. Hank bit the inside of his cheek to keep from moaning. Tafari's claws scored Hank's skin. His teeth sank into Hank's chest. A wild cry vibrated from Tafari's throat as hot cum filled the space between them. Tafari's asshole tried sucking Hank deeper. The air left Hank's lungs. He cried out as an orgasm ripped through him. Tafari's tongue filled his mouth again. This time, Hank kissed him back as he pumped Tafari's ass full of cum. He held Tafari tightly against him as his cock jumped, spitting out every drop. Even though he didn't understand how he had ended up like this, Hank relished the moment. He could and probably would have all the regrets later. But with his twitching dick in Tafari's ass, nothing felt wrong. In fact, it felt a hell of a lot like they had been written in the stars.

***

TAFARI FELT Hank's racing thoughts, but he had no regrets. Hank was his mate. If he waited for Hank to figure that out, they would both be old and gray.

"Why did you wait so long to come to me if you knew you belong with me?"

Hank's question surprised Tafari. He hadn't felt Hank's thoughts heading in that direction. Despite the mess between them, Tafari snuggled even closer. He had been alone for a long time. Physical touch was nice. "I've been watching you. You've never seemed interested in companionship. I didn't think you'd want me."

Hank held Tafari against his chest and rolled from the bed. He headed for the bathroom, leaving Tafari no choice but to wrap his legs around Hank's waist to keep from falling on the floor. Hank set him on the bathroom counter and snagged a clean washcloth from a nearby stack. He kept his gaze on wetting the cloth while Tafari stared at his serene expression.

Hank set to work cleaning Tafari. It was nice. "What made you decide tonight was the night?"

Tafari was lost in the peacefulness of Hank. His heartbeat was steady. Hank's hands were gentle on Tafari's skin. He felt cherished. That loosened his tongue. "Caspian found me in the woods and told me it was time."

That snagged Hank's full attention. His gaze locked on Tafari's. "So even Caspian knew you were out there, but I didn't."

It hit Tafari. The reason he couldn't read Hank's thoughts and feelings was because he hid them. But Tafari could hear the anger in Hank's voice, and he hated it. Tafari wasn't a delicate flower, though. He was a prickly beast. "You might've known if you hadn't forgotten me. If knowing was so damn important to you, maybe you could have thought about me occasionally." He shoved at Hank's chest before leaping from the counter. "You might have known I was right outside your door, if I had crossed your mind one goddamn time in the last twenty years. But

I guess I'm just not that important. Mates just don't count for what they used to, but don't worry. I'll get out if your hair and you can forget me again. I get that you're half human. That half can find someone new, I guess. Maybe I will too."

Before Tafari made it two steps, he found himself plucked off his feet and squashed against a huge chest. He fought to get away, scratching Hank's arms and trying to bite. Hank's mouth touched his ear. A low shushing sound cut through his rage. Warm lips caressed the shell of his ear.

"Stop." Hank kissed his neck. "Just listen." Hank kissed him again. "Please?"

Tafari fell still, but he stayed poised to fight. He didn't need anyone, even a mate. If Hank could forget him, Tafari could do the same.

Hank caressed him. "Shhh. Don't be angry. Back when I healed you, I was only a teenager. I knew I was different, and I had powers, but I didn't want to acknowledge them. Everyone thought I was strange, and I just wanted to fit in. I healed you because I couldn't stand to see you hurt. But I couldn't let myself acknowledge you were anything other than a cat. I didn't want to be different. I wanted friends. If you had stayed, though, I would've eventually figured things out. It took me a while to get to where I am mentally, but I don't care what anyone thinks anymore." He hugged Tafari tighter against his chest. "But I care what you think and how you feel. Please don't leave."

Tafari went limp. A small part of him wanted to apologize. The rest of Tafari was stubborn. He didn't want to admit he might have overreacted. Tafari sniffed. "You don't want me." His hurt slipped out without his permission.

"I do."

Tafari sniffed again at Hank's adamant-sounding claim. Hank carried him back to bed. Tafari didn't hesitate to cling to Hank as they settled beneath the covers. He felt like shit for clawing Hank's skin.

"Don't worry. It's already healed."

A smile tugged at Tafari's lips as he realized Hank had heard his thoughts. They were connected deeper than even Tafari had known. Tafari had found his home. He wouldn't lose it or Hank ever again.

Chapter Sixteen

EACH DAY, Tafari joined Hank at the liquor store. He always stayed in cat form. Mostly, he chose that form because he didn't want to get to know the townsfolk who had never noticed him before, but he also liked to judge everyone. Tafari stayed on the counter and inspected each purchase. Sometimes, he tolerated pets from certain customers. More than anything, he enjoyed staying in Hank's head, talking shit about everyone and what they bought. He liked the way Hank visibly fought back laughter at his antics.

Hank had given him a gorgeous collar. Tafari never took it off, not even in human form. It was a little loose on him in animal form, but he liked the way it draped his chest. Being adored was addictive. Three months under Hank's roof had him sickeningly in love. Tafari sneaked a peek at Hank while he stocked shelves. He had the sexiest arms. Tafari licked his lips. He wished they were alone. Thanks to the sprite who always hung out behind the counter, they were never alone at the store.

The door opened, bringing a cold breeze inside the store. Tafari glanced over his shoulder. Wade strolled in with his wolf... on a leash. Tafari had to investigate. He padded closer, sticking close to the wall so Charlie didn't eat him. Once he was within reach, he leaped onto the counter and peered over the edge at the wolf.

"Oh. Hey, Tafari. Where's Hank?" Wade asked as he stroked Tafari's head.

"He touched me. With his dog hands. Now I smell like dog."

A chuckle rang through Hank's mind as Hank moved to the front of the store. "I'm here. What can I help you with?"

A kind smile touched Wade's lips. He looked like a nice guy. Tafari would give him that. "Charlie and I were hoping you would come for dinner tonight. Tafari is invited too, of course," Wade added.

Tafari felt Hank's mixed feelings. On one hand, this was out of the blue and Wade had eaten his cat. Not that Wade knew Hank knew about that one. On the other hand, Hank had always secretly longed for at least one accepting friend in this town.

Hank stroked Tafari's back. He knew Hank silently asked his thoughts. *"Sure. Why not? We can fuck with him while he tries to keep his secret hidden from us."*

"Where's human Charlie?" Hank asked, making Tafari purr with satisfaction.

"He's at home. He had a bit of a migraine this morning. While he's feeling better now, he didn't think the cold would be good for his head.

"Mhmm. Well, I suppose if he's up for company, then Tafari and I can swing by after work."

A bright smile lit Wade's face. His overall countenance was one of kindness. Tafari supposed he passed the vibe check. *"Make sure he doesn't make me eat on the floor."*

"Tafari won't eat on the floor."

Wade never stopped smiling. He genuinely looked thrilled at the idea of Hank and Tafari coming for dinner. "That's not a problem. We'll see you a little after seven."

Hank nodded. "See you then."

The moment the pair disappeared, Tafari looked Hank's way.

Hank looked thoughtful. "What do you think that's all about?"

"Maybe he wants to admit he ate your last cat."

Hank shook his head. "I don't think so. He didn't seem nervous. I'd be nervous in that case if I was him."

Tafari didn't have any other ideas. It seemed they would soon find out. He just hoped they didn't regret this. Hank needed a friend, especially one who understood what it was like to love a Were. He had his paws crossed, for Hank's sake.

HANK KEPT Tafari in his arms as they walked through town. Even though most of the townsfolk loved to pet a domesticated wildcat when they were in the liquor store, outside Tafari made them nervous. Tafari was unbothered, but then Tafari was unruffled by most everything.

When they reached Wade's, the human version of Charlie let them inside. The young blond petted Tafari, greeting him before Hank. That was fine with Hank.

Finally, light blue eyes swung his way. "Hey, Hank. How are you?"

As much as Hank didn't care for people, he loved animals, and like Tafari, Charlie was more animal at heart than human. Hank softened. "Hey, Charlie. I'm fine. How are you?"

"I'm good. I hope you like steak. Wade cooked."

Hank nodded. "Steak sounds good. I didn't think to ask what I needed to bring, so I brought wine."

Charlie accepted the bottle without sparing it a glance. "Thank you. We just went grocery shopping, so we didn't need anything, but this was sweet." His gaze moved back Tafari's way. "I didn't know what you like, so we got you salmon. I hope that's okay."

"They did good."

Hank smiled as he set Tafari on the floor. Tafari sounded like he would withhold final judgment until he tasted the food. "That's great. Tafari loves fish."

Charlie turned away and motioned for them to follow. "Wade is setting the table."

Wade glanced up from his task as they stepped inside the kitchen. "Hey. I'm so glad you could make it." He pulled a chair out in front of a plate of salmon. "Here you go, Tafari. Your plate is already waiting."

Tafari leaped into the chair and settled down, patiently waiting for everyone else. Hank sat in the seat beside him and draped his arm across the back of the chair without thinking. For a half a second, he wondered how the move looked, then he mentally shrugged. Tafari's feelings meant more to him than Wade and Charlie's opinion.

"Everything smells delicious."

Wade uncovered the dishes in the center of the table. "Thank you. We went shopping earlier, and it reminded us we've been meaning to ask if you'd like to come over one night."

Hank didn't point out Wade had claimed Charlie had been in a bed with a migraine earlier. "I appreciate the invite. Admittedly, I don't get out much."

Charlie shrugged. "We're introverts, so we get it. Dig in. I know I'm starving."

As Hank snagged a steak, Tafari took a dainty bite of his salmon, as if trying to eat as cleanly as possible at the table.

Wade smiled and leaned forward, getting closer to Tafari. "Look at you. Such good table manners. Adorable."

Tafari curled his lip, showing his sharp teeth at the condescending compliment. "*Ask him where dog Charlie is. I want to watch him squirm.*"

"Where's dog Charlie?" Hank asked dutifully.

Wade and Charlie exchanged a glance. Wade answered. "He's locked in the bedroom."

"Doesn't he want to eat?" Hank felt no guilt.

Charlie looked longingly at his plate before moving to his feet. "I'll go see."

A minute passed after Charlie left the room before a huge white wolf trotted into the room. Wade fed him some steak from his plate.

Tafari's snicker rang through Hank's mind. *"Now who has table manners? Do they really think we can't see he's wearing the same damn collar as human Charlie?"*

Hank bit the inside of his cheek, trying to get his humor under control. "What happened to the other Charlie? I thought he was starved." Hank might have felt a little bad about tormenting them, but Wade had killed his old cat, Princess. Even though Hank knew it had been an accident, since Wade had lycan-thropy sickness. He couldn't control himself on nights when the moon was full, but still. Hank had loved that cat. She had been his baby. Wade didn't know Hank knew, and he had forgiven Wade months ago, but Hank couldn't resist a little revenge.

Wade stood. "I'll go see where he went."

Dog Charlie followed on Wade's heels down the hall. A minute later, Wade returned with human Charlie on his heels. His hair was a mess. No doubt from rapidly taking his shirt off and on and changing from wolf to human.

"Sorry about that. I hope you haven't been waiting for me."

Honestly, this had truly gone too far. Hank knew what it was like to be the outcast. He couldn't take it anymore. "For fuck's sake," Hank said, coming to his feet. He went to work, unbuttoning his flannel shirt. This whole thing was dumb and Tafari was miserable having to stay in cat form all the time—like he was some sort of secret. Tafari had been trying to keep those thoughts hidden from him since they'd arrived. That was the real reason Tafari enjoyed judging every customer that came in the store. It was a defense mechanism, hiding his hurt. Tafari felt like he had been right here, ignored and hidden away his entire life—unaccepted by anyone in this town. Hank couldn't take it anymore.

As Hank peeled off his shirt, Wade held up his hand. "Whoa. Hold up. We didn't invite you here for that."

Hank rolled his eyes and tossed the shirt over Tafari's back. "I'm not hiding you, baby. It's time to stop the charade."

In an instant, Tafari turned human. He quickly slipped his arms through the shirt and held it closed. He flashed a bright smile at Hank. "Thank you, baby."

"I knew it!" Charlie yelled at the top of his lungs. "I fucking knew it." He pointed at Wade. "Didn't I tell you? I told you he smelled like a Were."

Hank reclaimed his seat and went back to eating. He wasn't the excitable type. That was why he was a cat person. Dogs were dramatic.

Charlie visibly calmed and reclaimed his seat. Wade did too. Charlie focused on Tafari. "It's nice to finally meet you, Tafari. It's so damn nice to not be alone in this town."

Wade cast him a hurt look. "You're not alone."

Charlie patted his arm. "You know what I mean."

Tafari leaned closer to Hank. Hank pulled Tafari's chair closer and tucked him beneath his arm. He wasn't used to people seeing him like this, and Hank felt his nerves fraying. "It's nice to meet you both."

Charlie practically bounced in his seat. "Where did you come from? How long have you been here?"

Tafari started pushing on Hank's thigh like he was making bread, proving how much his discomfort grew. "I don't know, and as long as I can remember."

Charlie's eyebrows snapped together. "Where have you been hiding?"

Tafari shrugged and pressed harder on Hank's thigh. "I don't have to hide. No one notices me."

Hank pressed his lips to Tafari's temple. "*I don't know what anyone else notices, but I can't take my eyes off you. You have me completely mesmerized.*"

Tafari's muscles relaxed. "*I love you.*"

The breath caught in the back of Hank's throat. Hank was captivated by Tafari. He absolutely loved him, but they had never said the words. "I love you too."

Tafari's gaze snapped to Hank's as Hank said the words out loud. Hank held Tafari's stare. He wasn't ashamed. Tafari was his mate. They had been made for each other.

Caspian strolled into the kitchen like he lived there, bringing all eyes toward the doorway. His husband, Brock, was on his heels. They were quickly followed by the hardware store owner, Jack, and his husband Titan. Hank's eyebrows rose. Tafari wore nothing but Hank's flannel shirt and he hadn't known there were more people coming. He hadn't meant to expose Tafari to so many people.

"Oh good. We finally have everyone under one roof."

At Caspian's claim, Hank's gaze shot Wade's way. Since he had been the one to invite them, it seemed like he should be the one Hank blamed. Wade looked every bit as surprised as Hank.

"Uh. Hey, everyone. Why are you in my house?"

Caspian didn't look the least bit guilty for breaking and entering. "I saw you leave the liquor store and then I saw Hank and Tafari headed this way. I knew it was time." Without explaining what time it was, Caspian motioned Charlie's way. "Everyone, you already know Charlie. He's a werewolf." Charlie gasped at the way Caspian just dropped his secret in front of Jack and Titan. Caspian kept going like nothing happened. He motioned toward Tafari. "Tafari is the liquor store wildcat. Hank is half Fae." Everyone looked at him, except Tafari, who squeezed his knee. Hank forced a bland smile to his lips. He honestly didn't know how else to react to Caspian spilling his life-long secret.

Caspian motioned Titan's way. "Titan is a Gorgon and part of the Pantheon Council, and I'm a warlock. Now that all of that is out of the way, this town has a big problem and we're the only people with the knowledge and power to stop it."

Hank rubbed his forehead. As a Fae, he had known everyone's secrets. He spent enough time around the townsfolk—because everyone loved to drink—that he had picked up on their powers, even if he hadn't always been able to put a name to it. He had known the supernatural community had been growing inside their town, but that didn't mean he wanted to get dragged into any nonsense. They had never wanted to count him as one of their ranks. There was no need for them to start now.

"Just because I'm half Fae doesn't automatically mean I want to be part of some vigilante group."

Caspian's gaze moved to Hank. "I know you're bitter over being cast as the oddball in this town your entire life, but you live here too. Tafari lives here. If we don't do something about the failing of the magic safety net surrounding our border, we'll soon be overrun by God only knows what. You know this place is like a beacon of magical light. It's what drew me here. That's why Charlie, Titan, and Tafari are here. Yes, these are good men, but it's only a matter of time before the next new additions are not. We've already killed two zombies and a vampire. Those were only stragglers. If we get overrun by a healthy group all at once, this place won't stand a chance. It'll be wiped from the map with us in it."

It occurred to Hank that he had noticed a shift in the flow of magic lately. He hadn't realized it was this bad, though. Hank hadn't heard about zombies or vampires in their town. Tafari stroked his leg. Hank couldn't let anything happen to the love of his life. "What do you need me to do?"

Caspian gave him a sharp nod, showing his approval. He took a step back, and Brock motioned for Jack and Titan to do the same, giving Caspian space. Caspian closed his eyes. His chest expanded with a deep breath. When his eyes opened, they glowed bright green. The same glow flowed from his hands. Caspian's lips moved with a silent chant. He waved his hands, casting the glow outward until a green grid shaped every wall in the house before disappearing again. His hands and eyes went back to normal. He looked drained. Brock rubbed his back while Caspian explained.

"I just cast the same magical protection around this house that the entire town needs to have rebuilt. I'm only one person. There's no way I can do this alone." He winced. "I've been trying for months. So far, while working only late at night where no one will see, I've managed to shore up a quarter mile at the northeast border. Then I had to rest for two weeks because I had nothing left."

Hank got what he was saying, but he didn't know how two Weres, a Gorgon, and a Fae could help. Apparently, Wade felt the same because he was the first to speak. "What do you need from us? I don't know about anyone else, but I'm not a Warlock. As much as I'd love to help, I can't paint the town in a magic grid."

"Actually, you can," Caspian said, confusing Hank. "Everyone in this room has magic in their blood.

Even human mates are special. They carry a slice of magical soul that connects them to their mate. All I need is that grain of magic and I can teach you to do what I just did. Hank, you already can do magic. Your people helped build the invisible barrier around this town. Between the two of us, we could move mountains. I need your help."

As Caspian had pointed out, his whole life, Hank had been the outcast. Hank rarely used his powers. They were rusty and untrained. Everything he knew how to do, he had learned by accident or out of pure will. He didn't know if he could do this huge thing they were asking. His gaze moved to Tafari.

"You can do this. I know you can. You're already my hero."

Hank traced the shell of Tafari's ear. He couldn't risk anyone showing up in his town and harming his mate. Hank's life had been empty before Tafari. If anything happened to him, Hank wouldn't survive it. The three months they had been together may as well have been thirty years. There was no deeper attachment than true soulmates. As Caspian had said, they carried a slice of each other's actual soul. They weren't whole apart. *"I love you."*

"*I love you too.*"

Hank took a deep breath. "Okay. Just let me know when you want to get started." Hank prayed he wasn't making the biggest mistake of his life by joining this ragtag group of creatures. For his wildcat, there was nothing he wouldn't do. Hank's heart was finally complete. He wouldn't lose it.

Chapter Seventeen

WARM LIPS BRUSHED the back of his neck. Tafari's eyes fell closed. He never grew tired of Hank's touch. With Hank helping Caspian each night after the liquor store closed, it felt like they never had any time alone. The four months since Tafari moved in with Hank had been a whirlwind. In some ways, it felt like they hadn't been given the bonding time they needed to thrive. Tafari tried not to lose himself to the sensation of Hank's lips on his skin. He knew nothing could come of it. They still had an hour before the store closed and then they would be back to drawing spells all night. He didn't want to feel cheated. Tafari knew this was a temporary state, but still. All he wanted was a normal life and it kind of pissed him off sometimes that he had to do all this for a town that didn't give a damn about him.

Hank drew Tafari down an aisle out of sight of the door. A smile tugged at the corners of Tafari's mouth. He would take any quality time with Hank he could get. Tafari braced his hand on the shelf beside him and sucked air through his nose, hoping to keep his body under control while Hank nibbled on his neck. Love and happiness filled Tafari's chest. He wished time would stop and let him savor this moment. He was so fucking in love that it never stopped wowing him.

"That's better," Hank whispered against his neck. "You're not allowed to be unhappy with me."

Guilt washed over Tafari. "I'm not. I swear." Tafari stroked Hank's chest, trying to distract him from those thoughts. He finally had the man he had dreamed of his entire life. Tafari would not allow Hank an ounce of regret for loving him.

"Oh, sorry. Hey, Tafari. I didn't mean to interrupt."

Tafari spun and blinked rapidly at Clara's sudden appearance. He always tried to stay in cat form inside the liquor store, but he had started wearing a long t-shirt so he could shift and steal any alone moments he could with Hank without walking around nude. Clara had never seen him when he wasn't a cat. She shouldn't even know him much less recognize him. In fact, she should be freaking the fuck out. Instead, she acted as if she saw him every day.

"I just wanted to stop by and give you two an invitation to my wedding."

With shock still rendering him mute, Tafari accepted the envelope Clara held out to him.

Hank didn't seem to suffer from the same level of surprise. "So Scott finally worked up the nerve to tie you down. That's amazing."

Clara made a dismissive motion. "Scott? Please. He's way too shy. I told him we were getting married. He blushed and said okay. Can I count on you two to be there?"

"Of course," Tafari said, sounding as blown away as he felt.

With a bright smile, Clara gave them a quick wave. "Cool. Gotta go. I have a ton of invites to deliver."

Tafari nodded and watched Clara head to the front. She knocked on the countertop as she passed. "See you later, Relic. Your name is on the invitation too."

Relic's tiny head popped up from behind the counter. "See you, lady. I'll be there."

Tafari slowly turned and met Hank's gaze. "What just happened?"

Hank shrugged. "This is a weird town full of strange people. Clara is just one of those people who believes in everything she can't see. That's probably exactly why she can see everything most people can't."

Tafari blinked slowly, trying to absorb the last few minutes. "Holy shit. Do you mean I could actually have a normal life here someday? The way Charlie does? Maybe not exactly the way Charlie does, but you know what I mean."

Hank shrugged. "I don't see why not. People think I'm odd, but they haven't come after me with pitch-forks. Who knows? Maybe one day, everyone in town will learn the truth and you can choose to shift wherever and whenever you want."

That sounded like an amazing dream. Still, he shrugged, refusing to let that hope take root. "As long as I have you, I'm good. If I get to be free, then great. If not, then I'm still happier than I've ever been."

"Hey, Tafari."

Tafari spun again at the sound of his name. The butcher, Ben, from the grocery store headed down the aisle. "We were closing up tonight and we had this leftover salmon. My wife hates it, so she suggested I stop by and leave it with you, if you're interested?"

On one hand, Tafari was hyperaware he only wore a long t-shirt. But mostly, Tafari had no fucking clue what was happening with his life. "Oh. Um. Thank you." He passed Clara's invitation to Hank and accepted the salmon. "I really appreciate it."

Ben nodded. "It's no problem. I'd better get home. Jamie is waiting."

"Okay. Tell her I said hi."

Ben nodded. "Will do." He headed for the door. Before Tafari could look Hank's way to commiserate again, Samantha from the second-hand store was there. "Hey, Tafari. I got some new donations in today, and I found this outfit." She held up a gorgeous romper. "I thought of you. This would be so cute on you no matter what form you're in. Don't you think?"

"Okay. That's adorable, but what's happening?" There was already two more people waiting behind Samantha and Tafari recognized a planned conspiracy when he saw one.

Samantha shrugged. "The townsfolk have just been thinking and talking. Hank and you have been sacrificing so much for us by trying to shore up the magic barrier around town and you haven't even been given a proper welcome. Everyone feels super guilty for making Charlie and you feel like you have to hide."

"You know about the magic and Charlie too?" Tafari sounded weak—like he might faint. He honestly thought he might.

Samantha made a dismissive gesture. "Anyone who's lived in Elvenwood more than a week knows this place has something special. Anyhow, I have a roast in my crockpot back home, so I need to get going. Plus, you have a line of people waiting to meet you."

She passed Tafari the romper. "Come see me at the shop sometime. I bet I can find a ton of stuff that'll make your shifting easier, clothing wise."

Tafari clasped the outfit to his chest. He wondered if he would cry. "Thank you."

As person after person stopped by to bring him a gift, Tafari felt a shift in his chest. Hank kept rubbing his back and Tafari felt the pride for Tafari and this town that rolled from Hank. Tafari realized the townsfolk weren't only showing Tafari their acceptance. They were embracing Hank through Tafari. Tafari looked Hank's way. They held each other's stare as they came to a silent agreement. This place was worth it. Every sacrifice and late night, until they were fully protected, these people deserved their time. As much as neither of them had ever wanted to admit it, they loved this place. They would fight for Elvenwood. This was where their love had been born. They would thrive here and live out their lives here without having to hide. It was the most beautiful place in the world to them for that fact alone. They would devote their lives to each other and this town. It sounded like a worthy life to him. A happy life.

Introduction to Witchin Fangs

With the town's supernatural community trying to shore up the magic wall around their borders, they're getting overwhelmed. They need someone who moves fast and is awake all night. Caspian knows just the guy.

When Stefan agreed to leave his beloved hometown of New Orleans to move to a tiny town in the middle of Ohio, Caspian could have warned him the place was full of sprites. Those tiny, magical creatures are Stefan's favorite flavored juice box. The scent drives him wild. Luckily, there's one spitfire of a sprite willing to keep his cravings satisfied. Now all he can do is hope he doesn't end up getting precious Relic killed.

Witchin Fangs is the fifth book in Charity Parkerson's Witchin series. These fun, short paranormal romances are meant to be devoured on your lunch break. Read along as a tiny town in Ohio grows its supernatural community one resident at a time.

Chapter Eighteen

WHILE SPENDING each night helping to shore up the magical borders of Elvenwood could get pretty boring, such was life for Relic. As a sprite, he didn't know if he made a huge dent in the work. After all, he was just a little guy. Eight inches, to be precise. He could make himself human-sized, but then all his magic went to being bigger and he had nothing left to work side-by-side with his fellow supernatural brethren. It was a conundrum. Sometimes, he wondered if he helped at all, but he still kept showing up. It was the least he could do for the place where he had lived his entire life.

Elvenwood, Ohio was a tiny town surrounded by magical woods. The area was exactly as the name suggested: Elven woods. Centuries ago, Elves had made this place their home. They had fortified the area with a magical safety net, keeping out any creatures with bad intentions. The elves had fortified the land, making it flourish with life and luck. The happiness and blessings were plentiful. Magic pulsed from the town, casting a beacon of invisible light that drew anyone with as much as a drop of magical blood their way. In the past, if a creature had malice in their heart, they would sense the magic but wander aimlessly as the town stayed hidden from them, just out of sight.

Unfortunately, time passed and changed, as time does. The elves wandered, and Elvenwood had been forgotten by the creatures who had founded it. The magic had begun to fade over the years, leaving its residents defenseless against evil. That was how the supernatural townsfolk had ended up here, acting as magical masons to the invisible barrier. The first few nights, Relic had worked on his own, getting nowhere. After that, Relic realized he was more help if he stayed in his friend Hank's shirt pocket. Hank was half Fae and owned the liquor store where Relic lived. They had discovered, if Relic loaned his power to Hank, then Hank could work two more hours each night. Hank could cover more ground in two hours than Relic could all night. They were trying to work smarter, not harder, but still. Sometimes, Relic felt very small in the face of so much. He wanted to do more. Relic just didn't know how.

He stayed lost in his negative thoughts as he fed Hank his powers. His skin itched tonight. Relic stirred, becoming more aware of their surroundings as the itch became almost unbearable. The hair stood on the back of his neck. Something inside him urged him to run. He didn't feel safe any longer.

"Something is coming."

Hank stopped mid chanting of spells. His dark blue gaze dropped to where Relic chilled in his pocket. "What's wrong?"

Relic rubbed the back of his neck, trying to wipe away the chill. "I don't know. Something is wrong."

Hank's mate, Tafari, stuck his nose in the air and sniffed. As a Werecat, his senses were more heightened than anyone else there. His eyes glowed amber, proving how close he was to shifting. "He's right.

There's something..." He sniffed again. His gaze shot to the sky. Something moved in the air, blending with the darkness. Tafari's eyes glowed brighter. His features turned more catlike by the second. Relic was fascinated by the way his stance changed. Tafari leaped into the air, transforming into an Asian leopard cat, and snatching something from the sky. When they hit the ground, it was with a bigger thud than Relic expected. It was a man. Tafari's deadly jaw was locked tightly around their intruder's throat.

"Whoa. Whoa. Whoa. I'm a friend of Caspian's. He asked me to come here and help."

A terrifying, low growl vibrated from Tafari's throat. Relic wondered if he was about to witness a murder.

"Remind me not to sneak up on you," he whispered to Hank. Relic hadn't realized how deadly Tafari could be.

Hank made a soothing noise. "It's okay, Tafari. You can let go."

At Hank's urging, Tafari backed away and shifted back into a man.

Relic gave him a thumbs-up. "Those rompers are really working out for you. Nary a naked dick was seen."

Tafari blushed and stroked the cotton romper he wore. "This really has worked out well. I'm so glad Samantha suggested these for shifting."

The man on the ground rolled to his knees and brushed the dirt from his clothes as he stood. "Oh, are we discussing fashion now that I've been assaulted?"

Tafari flounced in a way that made Relic smile. It was exactly like Tafari had twitched his tail at the new arrival, even though he was in human form. "You shouldn't sneak up on people in the dark."

Hank, always the calm voice of reason, chimed in. "Caspian didn't tell us to expect anyone. What's your name?"

The man's swirling, dark gaze landed on Hank before it dropped to Relic. The tips of his fangs appeared. Relic sank deeper into Hank's pocket. "I'm Stefan." He sounded distracted. His gaze never wavered from where Relic stayed half hidden. "Is that a sprite in your pocket, or am I just very happy to see you?"

Relic rolled his eyes. "Great. Caspian's not only sent us a vampire. The guy's a dumbass."

"I'm a dumbass with excellent hearing." Stefan moved closer.

Relic ducked lower.

Tafari released another warning growl.

Stefan shook his head. "Apologies. Sprite blood is very enticing. It tastes like candy and makes vampires euphoric."

"Don't let him bite me, Hank. I'm a little guy. He'd shrivel me up like drinking a juice box."

"I won't bite you, little one. As I said, I'm here to help. Not cause trouble. Caspian told me about the town's failing defenses. Since I'm awake all night and can move at three times the speed of a normal magical being, I've come to lend my wings."

Relic peeked over the edge of the flannel that hid him from sight. "I'd like to see the wings."

Stephan dutifully turned. A set of bat wings expanded from his expensive-looking jacket. They flapped twice before disappearing again.

He had Tafari's attention. "How did you do that through your clothes? That's a neat trick."

A secretive-looking smirk touched Stefan's lips. "Vampires are full of alluring magic. Everything about us is meant to seduce prey." His gaze flickered to Relic again. "We have lots of tricks to get what we want." Stefan switched his gaze to the sky. "Unfortunately, the dawn approaches. I must find a place to rest. Tomorrow night, I'll join you and maybe we can have this border painted in new spells in no time. *Au revoir.*"

Relic was fascinated. He wasn't ready for the vampire to disappear. He liked the man's accent. "I live in the cellar at Hank's liquor store. There aren't any windows. You'd be safe down there from the sunlight." Relic knew he was an idiot for offering, but they needed the help. The least they could do was offer Stefan a place to stay.

Humor lit Stefan's features. "That's sweet, sprite, but I'm sure you won't feel safe with me."

Relic's irritation spiked. "I have a name, and I was only trying to be nice. Find your own damn place to stay, then, but good luck. You have less than an hour until sunrise and the only hotel has so many windows, it may as well be made of glass."

Stefan gave him a slight bow. "It seems I owe you another apology. May I have your name?"

Relic sniffed. "It's Relic."

"Nice to meet you, Relic. If you're quite certain you'll feel safe with me, I'd be honored to stay with you. You have my word you'll come to no harm. As delicious as you smell, I'm very old. I can control myself."

Relic disappeared and reappeared on Stefan's shoulder. "How old is very old?"

Stefan didn't look surprised to find Relic using his shoulder as a bench. "Seven hundred and twenty-three, this year."

"Oooh. It's so rare for me to meet anyone older than me. The liquor store is a mile from here, if you'd like to get going."

"I could fly us, if you point the way."

Relic fought an excited laugh. "I would love that."

"Are you sure you'll be okay?"

Hank's question caught Relic off guard. He had nearly forgotten him. "Yes. I'll be fine. If any fangs head my way, I can just disappear."

Hank looked a bit skeptical, but he nodded. "All right. Zap back to me if you need me."

Relic nodded and immediately forgot Hank again. "I'm three hundred and ninety-one this year. There's no one left around these parts as old as me."

Stefan held his hand out for Relic. "Let me hold you so you don't fall." The moment Relic was securely in Stefan's grasp, Stefan's feet left the ground. The wind ruffled Relic's hair. Stefan kept up his end of the conversation. "Are there no other sprites in these woods? I'd think with magic as deeply rooted as it is in this town, sprites would sprout everywhere."

Relic nodded. "There are quite a few younger than me, but most of the others my age or older were wiped out in the great flood about a hundred years ago. We'd had a grand celebration that day and so many of my kind had fallen over drunk off honeysuckle. Then the flood came and wiped them out in their sleep."

Stefan looked engrossed. "That's terrible. How did you survive?"

"Turn left here. That's the liquor store right there with the bright red sign. I don't like honeysuckle. It's too sweet."

A sexy chuckle rumbled from Stefan and took Relic by surprise. Stefan was a vampire. Relic had heard horror stories about vampires wiping out entire fields of sprites. Stefan didn't feel like a monster, though. He seemed kind of nice. Relic focused on the last few seconds of flying, enjoying the moment before Stefan's feet hit the ground. The second they landed, Relic zapped from Stefan's hand to the ground and grew to his human size, so he could let them in.

"That's a neat trick."

Relic flashed Stefan a smile. "My turn to transport you my way." He snagged Stefan's arm and pulled Stefan through space and time, landing inside his cellar home.

A loud laugh burst from Stefan. "Are you telling me you could've zapped us directly here?"

Relic shrugged. "Yes, but I've never flown before. I didn't want to miss my chance."

A sweet smile touched Stefan's features. "I am at your service should you like to go again."

Something tickled Relic's gut—like butterflies playing in his stomach. Relic returned to his usual size in his discomfort. Stefan was very pretty. He was pale, but his black eyes reflected the light, mesmerizing Relic. Relic kind of wanted to touch the short, soft-looking brown curls on Stefan's head to see if they were as fluffy as they looked. He needed to get back to his comfort zone.

"Um. This is my place."

Stefan looked away and inspected the cellar. "It'll definitely be dark enough, but I don't really see a place for me to sleep."

They both stared at Relic's tiny bed. It was definitely meant for an eight-inch-tall man.

Relic snapped his fingers, and the bed became queen-sized. "There. All better." He pointed toward the bathroom. "The bathroom is through there. If you need anything, I can create most anything for you, as long as it's natural materials."

"I'm good." Stefan opened his jacket, revealing a small, thin backpack beneath. "I have everything I need for an overnight stay. My luggage is supposed to arrive at Caspian's shop tomorrow."

Relic nodded. "That's good. I'm surprised Caspian didn't offer to let you stay with him since you came here to do him a favor."

"He did."

Relic held Stefan's stare. He didn't know how to react to that revelation. "Oh."

Stefan's smile grew. "Do you care if I steal the bathroom first or would you like the first go?"

Relic shrugged. "Go ahead. I can wait."

With a wink, Stefan headed inside the bathroom. Relic stared at the closed door like a deer trapped in headlights. He had no clue what he had gotten himself into. Relic just prayed he lived through the night.

A SPRITE. Stefan shook his head. It had been ages since he had seen one of those. He definitely had never chatted with one. It had been an interesting evening. Learning sprites could make themselves man-sized had been a pleasant surprise. Relic was enchanting. Everything inside the bathroom was built for a human. Stefan imagined that was because of Hank, since Relic's bed had been sprite-sized. Since Stefan didn't eat, and the blood he drank became the energy he burned, he didn't need the bathroom beyond changing tonight. He had been slightly tempted to strip in front of Relic just to see him flustered. But Stefan needed Relic to be comfortable and compliant.

"Have you reached Elvenwood?"

The voice inside his head startled him. After seven hundred years, he should be accustomed to the sudden intrusions, but he wasn't. *"Yes."*

"Have you met any of the community there?"

"I have."

A menacing feeling had goosebumps rising on his skin. He also hated when Magnus' emotions overwhelmed his. Every vampire had this bond with their maker. For some, it could be pleasant, even sensual. For Stefan, it was the occasional nightmare as Magnus stormed into his life again after centuries of silence.

"Do they suspect you?"

Stefan fought an eye roll. *"Why should they suspect me of anything? I've been here fifteen minutes and Caspian invited me. The sun is rising. I must find a safe place for the day."*

"Keep me posted."

"I will."

Stefan felt Magnus retreat. He spent a minute swallowing down the bitterness. Stefan was too old for regrets. Life was what it was, but sometimes the resentment hit from nowhere, flaring his temper. With a deep breath, Stefan put his game face on and opened the bathroom door. He didn't see Relic right away. Finally, he spotted Relic's tiny form curled up on one of the pillows, sound asleep. Stefan smiled as he moved toward the bed. Relic slept peacefully, obviously sure of his safety. The knowledge caused a pang in Stefan's chest. No one should trust him or any other vampire, for that matter. They lived for one thing only: blood.

Stefan turned away and found the light switch. After plunging the room into darkness, he returned to the bed. He eased beneath the covers, doing his best not to disturb the sleeping sprite. Once he was settled on his side, Stefan stared at Relic. He had perfect vision, even in the dark. Relic was mesmerizing. He was pure magic. Untainted by evil or humans. Relic was the closest thing to an angel on Earth Stefan had ever met. He was beautiful. Auburn hair and clear green eyes. There was a light smattering of freckles across the bridge of his nose. If Stefan had met Relic as a human, he would likely pursue him harder than any man ever had. But there was no humanity left in Stefan and he could only pretend to be decent.

Relic shivered in his sleep. Stefan automatically pulled the corner of the comforter up and covered him. Relic released a contented sigh. Stefan smiled at the sound and closed his eyes. The sun was coming. He could feel it slowing his heart and stealing his strength. Soon he would disappear into his daytime death. Despite knowing he couldn't dream, Stefan still hoped he would. If he could, he would dream of Relic and his kindness. No one had shown him this much trust in centuries. It felt good. Stefan wished for more.

Chapter Nineteen

BY THE TIME NIGHT FELL, the liquor store was closed again, and Relic was gone. Stefan hated this time of year. Even though the nights hadn't turned extremely cold for the year, he was awake for fewer hours. That would soon change with the time, but that hadn't happened yet. Even though he had an eternity to live, he was oddly excited to see Relic again, and the daylight hours had stolen him away. After dressing, Stefan immediately took to the skies and headed in the same direction as last night. He easily found the same group of men working on the magic grid. This time, Caspian was there as well.

As Stefan's feet hit the ground, Caspian closed the distance between them, smiling. He embraced

Stefan while slapping Stefan's back like an old friend. "It's so good to see you. It feels like forever."

"That's because it has been," Stefan said, patting Caspian's back. He stepped back and eyed Caspian. His brown eyes held a light Stefan didn't remember from their years in New Orleans. "You look good. Happy."

"That's because I am." Caspian motioned toward the other people present. "You've already met everyone, right? Hank said you showed up right before sunrise."

Stefan glanced Hank's way. "Yes. I don't think I caught everyone's name, but we met. Thank you for allowing me the use of your cellar, Hank."

Hank dipped his chin. "That's thanks to Relic, really, but you're welcome."

Stefan fought the urge to ask where Relic was hiding. "Nonetheless." He went back to focusing on Caspian. "Where is this man who's stolen you from the loving arms of *la belle* New Orleans? I must look him over and judge him accordingly."

"He's at home. Brock works a human job and I try to keep his life as normal as possible. I just wanted to see you before I head home."

Before Stefan could stop himself, he hugged Caspian again. They had become friends back when Caspian lived in the French Quarter of New Orleans. Few people outside of vampires socialized with their species, but Caspian had never treated Stefan any different. Stefan hadn't realized how much he had missed his friend before now. "Truly, it's so good to see you. We will catch up soon. Tonight, I will try to do as much of the border as possible. Maybe we can get this knocked out, no?"

Caspian nodded. "I hope so. Admittedly, we're all pretty wiped out. We've been at this nonstop for months. There's just not enough of us, and there are only so many hours in the day."

Stefan squeezed Caspian's shoulder. "Don't fret, my friend. I'm here." His gaze swept over Hank and Hank's Were mate. They looked every bit as exhausted as Caspian claimed. "You two should take the night off. I've got this."

They exchanged glances. The wildcat looked a bit suspicious. "If you're sure..."

Stefan nodded. "Go. Rest. This is why I am here. You need help and I have it to give."

Relic peered over the edge of Hank's pocket. "I can stay with him and loan him my magic. We could get a lot done between us."

A smile snapped to Stefan's lips. "Hello, poppet. If you're well rested, then I'd love the company."

Hank looked skeptical.

Caspian chimed in, "That's a great idea. Hank and Tafari deserve some time to relax."

Stefan wouldn't lose his chance to have more time alone with Relic. He held his hand out, palm up, and Relic jumped through time and space to land on his hand. Stefan set him on his shoulder.

Relic flashed him a sweet smile and something expanded inside Stefan's chest. Relic genuinely seemed happy to see him. He felt like a friend already. Stefan hadn't had a real one of those in a long time. Caspian didn't count. As much as Stefan liked Caspian, he felt the way Caspian held a small part of himself back from Stefan. Caspian never forgot Stefan was dangerous, which was fair, but still. Stefan missed having genuine friendships.

"Shall we get started, poppet?"

Relic nodded.

Everyone said their goodbyes.

Stefan called upon the magic inside him and drew on the power of his ancestors. Protection spells easily flowed from his fingertips. He swiped through the air.

"So you're pretty old."

Relic's sudden observation pulled a laugh from Stefan. "Thanks for that."

Relic shrugged. "It's just math, and nothing more, but you must know a lot. I mean, I'm old and I know a lot. I can't imagine how much more you know. You've probably been everywhere. I've never left this town. So I only know the stories I've been told about everything around the world and the creatures in it. I bet you've seen everything."

Stefan shrugged. "I suppose I likely have. Hold on to my jacket." Stefan sped, moving at three times the speed of a normal running human. He cast spells as he went, tossing up a barrier and strengthening the existing border. He lost himself to his task while Relic held on to his shoulder like his ass had been stuck with tape. Stefan's speed seemed not to faze him.

"You've been there for almost twenty-four hours. I've should've had a report by now."

"Give me more time. I'm asking questions now."

"What was that?"

"What?" Stefan asked, trying to sound innocent. He didn't think Relic could hear the voices in his head, but then again, Stefan didn't know what secret powers Relic possessed.

"You startled like you'd been zapped by electricity and then slowed down."

Stefan decided honesty would get him the furthest. "My maker. His voice occasionally burst into my head. It's a bit annoying and always shocking. A lot like someone bursting into your home unannounced,

I imagine."

Relic sat forward. He looked fascinated. "Your maker? Do you mean you were once human?"

Stefan nodded. "All living vampires were made. Only the very first came from a demon's curse. The rest of us were turned."

"Wow." Relic sounded blown away. "But you have wings and humans don't have wings. I wouldn't think humans could just have wings after being given what's basically a virus. For example, werewolves. We have a werewolf in town and his mate only suffers lycanthropy sickness after being bitten. He goes feral with full moons, but he doesn't change into a wolf, because he's human. He can't just be a wolf."

"It's only magic," Stefan said, trying to explain. "The wings aren't real. It's just a trick. That's why they don't rip through my clothes when they appear. Take, for example, your ability to disappear and reappear in a different spot. You're not actually disappearing. You still exist. It's just a trick of the light combined with time and speed. It's not real. I'm the same. Everything about me is an illusion."

"But you have fangs."

"That's evolution. Survival," Stefan explained. "I got bitten. I basically died. My incisors fell out, and I had working fangs by morning. Everything about me sped and heightened, ensuring survival. That includes the magic that was dormant in my blood. It grew and took over, making me capable of things an ordinary human could never do. If there had been no magic in my blood, I would've simply died when Magnus drained me. Hell, there would be vampires on every corner, otherwise. We would be the dominant species if everyone could turn. It takes magic."

Relic looked thoughtful, as if he turned inward.

Stefan pretended to focus solely on building the wall as he contacted Magnus. *"They have werewolves."*

"Werewolves. Fuck. Find out how many. That sets us back."

"I will try. It sounds like there are quite a few. It appears they may have beat us to the punch." It was a lie, of course, but the more time he spent with Relic; the guiltier Stefan felt about Magnus' plan to seize Elvenwood for his coven. Stefan had never wanted to be part of this. He couldn't disobey his maker. Stefan

wished Caspian had never called him. Then Magnus would have no reason to use him.

"I'll start planning a way around the wolves. You just keep the information coming."

"What about Caspian?" Relic asked out of the blue.

"What about him?" Stefan's mind had been so torn, he lost the threads of their conversation.

"He can see the future. That's more tangible than an illusion. Everything with a consciousness can make choices, changing every nuance of every possible outcome. How can he see people's exact future if it's ever-changing? I've always wondered that."

Stefan shook his head. "The future isn't ever-changing. We might think we have choices, and maybe we do, but they all lead to the same place. Our fates are set the moment we take our first breath. From there, we're all just puppets on a string being pulled to our inevitable demise."

"That's a pretty depressing way to look at things."

"It's just the truth of things." A wave of unexpected weariness washed over Stefan. "I need to sit down for a moment."

Relic eyed him as Stefan sat on the ground.

Stefan's chest felt heavy. His breathing shallowed. Exhaustion had his head spinning. He hoped he didn't pass out and fry when the sun rose. Then again, maybe that was for the best. Maybe that was the fate he had been getting pulled toward his entire life. A fitting end, he supposed.

RELIC EYED STEFAN. He didn't look so good. His skin was paler than usual, and his features were pinched. Relic had been loaning his magic to Stefan, but it didn't look like it was enough.

"Are you okay?"

Stefan nodded. "I haven't fed tonight. It's no big deal. Give me a moment. It'll pass."

A small part of Relic recognized he should fear being alone with a starved vampire. Instead, he was just worried about Stefan. Stefan had been kind to him. He had answered all of Relic's annoying questions and given away more about himself than Relic imagined he had meant to share. Stefan was bitter and unhappy. Relic doubted Stefan planned to expose that part of himself, but Relic heard the pain behind his words. He had never been more curious about anyone.

Stefan closed his eyes and took several deep breaths.

Relic stroked his cheek. His skin was like ice. Fear shot through Relic. He didn't understand why Stefan was so weak. "When was the last time you fed?"

A tired-looking smile touched Stefan's lips. It slipped away as quickly as it came. "A few days. Caspian asked me not to drink from anyone here."

Relic's temper spiked. "He asked for your help and then told you to starve. That's not what friends do."

Stefan didn't look outraged, and Relic didn't understand why. Caspian shouldn't have expected so much while denying Stefan the most basic of necessities to live. Stefan seemed to accept he was worthy of nothing more. "He doesn't want me upsetting the townsfolk. I understand. People like me aren't meant to mix with people like you."

Relic reeled at the words. He popped from Stefan's shoulder to the ground and turned human-sized. "What's that supposed to mean?"

Stefan didn't open his eyes, proving how exhausted he truly was. "You're good and pure. My kind lurk in the dark, preying on human blood. You bring light to the world. I drain life. We're not the same."

That broke Relic's heart. He felt Stefan's kindness, even if Stefan couldn't. He stroked Stefan's arm and took his hand. "You can drink from me."

Swirling dark eyes finally fixed upon him. "I can't ask that of you."

"You didn't."

Stefan's gaze openly begged Relic to take it back. "I don't want you to be afraid of me. You will be if I bite you."

Relic shook his head. "I won't. I trust you."

Stefan's chest quickly expanded and then caved as if Relic's words had punched him. "You shouldn't."

A bright smile exploded across Relic's face. "Too late. I've made my mind up about you. So how do we do this?"

Stefan still looked torn. He blinked several times, as if trying to wrap his mind around Relic's insanity. "Um. Well, look into my eyes."

Relic gave Stefan a sharp nod and moved to his knees. He made a show of focusing on Stefan's eyes. The moment he did, his mind went hazy. Then Stefan's lips touched his throat. Relic hadn't seen him move, but Relic wasn't afraid. Stefan's fangs pierced Relic's skin. A moan tore from Relic's throat. It was completely out of his control. No one had warned him. Maybe it was for the best. If Relic had known his body would respond like he experienced the first thrust of getting fucked, he might have spent his life hunting vampires and begging them to take his blood. Stefan sucked. Relic saw stars. He shrank before he could stop it from happening. It was like his bones were gelatin.

"Thank you, poppet."

Stefan scooped him from the ground and dropped him into the inside pocket of his jacket. He went back to casting spells like he hadn't stolen Relic's soul. Relic was speechless in the face of discovery. He had liked that and wanted to do it again. That was one secret he would likely take to his grave. Funny how that didn't feel wrong.

Chapter Twenty

THIS TIME, as the sun dipped low and the liquor store closed, Relic didn't opt to leave with Hank. Instead, he stayed in bed with Stefan and watched him sleep. He was peaceful. Relic felt a little guilty for staring, but he couldn't stop. Last night, even before the orgasmic experience of Stefan sucking his neck, Relic had enjoyed himself more than he had in years. No one sat and talked to him, especially since Hank had fallen for Tafari. Obviously, Relic adored Tafari, and he was happy for Hank, but Relic had lost his only friend when Tafari had arrived. They were wrapped up in each other and Relic was just that sprite who lived in Hank's cellar. He didn't have a purpose or friends. Life was a little too quiet. Last night, it hadn't been.

Stefan's eyes opened, catching Relic staring. "Hi."

Relic fought a smile. "Hi."

Stefan glanced around the room, as if gathering his bearings before meeting Relic's gaze again. "You waited for me."

"I thought maybe I had better feed you tonight before you almost fall out." Relic tried to keep his tone bland. He didn't want to sound desperate for Stefan's intoxicating fangs, but he was.

A sexy smile stretched Stefan's lips. "Careful. Your blood is delicious. You'll have me addicted."

Relic was a little ashamed of how quickly he turned human-sized, hoping to do exactly what Stefan feared. He didn't know why, but he liked the idea of Stefan desiring him in some way, even if it was only his blood. Relic scooted closer. "I'm magic. I can keep you satisfied." Honestly, he hadn't meant his words to sound quite so sexual. He didn't take them back.

The way Stefan looked at him left no doubt Stefan knew exactly what Relic wanted. Stefan's tongue shot out, wetting his bottom lip. Relic had never wanted to taste anything as badly in his life. Stefan didn't move closer. In fact, he didn't look like he planned to bite Relic at all.

"I need to tell you something."

Fuck. He was married. Relic knew that tone. He was about to get his feelings crushed. "Okay."

Stefan licked his bottom lip again. Relic could practically feel Stefan's nerves fraying. He took a ragged-sounding breath. "My maker sent me here to check out your town's defenses so he could plan a takeover."

Relic blinked. That was the last thing he had expected to hear. "Oh." He sat up. Before he ran away, the way he wanted, Stefan touched his arm. That one gesture held him in place even though Stefan wasn't trying.

"I don't want what he wants, but I can't disobey my maker. My blood is tied to his and will be as long as he lives. I have no choice but to obey. He can literally overtake my will and force me to do whatever he wants. I can't stop him."

Every word he spoke was the truth. Stefan didn't want to betray anyone. The truth was in his eyes. Relic moved without thinking. He pressed his lips to Stefan's in a quick kiss. Then he held Stefan's stare. "Don't worry. Everything will be okay. You can't disobey, but I can."

Relic started to move away. He needed to talk to Caspian. They had to come up with a plan. Stefan snagged the back of Relic's head before he got away. He claimed Relic's mouth. Relic's breath left him as Stefan's tongue stroked his. His heart beat too fast. Stefan rolled, pinning Relic beneath him. Relic clung to Stefan's bare chest and prayed Stefan didn't pull away. He had never felt less alone.

Stefan ran his hand down Relic's body. He lifted Relic's knee. Their bodies molded so perfectly, Relic's eyes burned with longing. He always tried to not want things for himself. He wanted this. The yearning was so fast and deep, it was almost unnatural. Relic had lived a long time. No one had ever made him feel so much.

Stefan pressed his forehead to Relic's. "I don't want you to get hurt because of me."

Relic's hands automatically tightened on Stefan's body. "I'm not as delicate as you think." And he would rather die than miss this chance. Being alone had already been slowly killing him anyhow. "You should take my blood. You'll need your strength."

Stefan nodded. He kissed a path to Relic's neck. Relic closed his eyes and savored every second. This time, when Stefan's fangs pierced Relic's skin, he knew what to expect. That still didn't stop Relic from gasping. He moved restlessly against Stefan. Relic felt Stefan's cock harden. The feeling of being powerful overtook him. If he could make this beautiful man lust, then he could do anything.

"I want you inside me."

Stefan sucked.

Relic pushed at Stefan's pajama pants, needing more. A growl of frustration rang through his head. He used his magic to make their clothes disappear. The neediest sound Relic had ever heard vibrated from Stefan against his throat as their nude bodies met. Relic didn't care if he seemed desperate. He was.

Stefan pulled away. He stared down at Relic, looking every bit as turned on as Relic felt. "I don't want to take advantage of you."

"You're not."

For a moment, Stefan's gaze searched Relic's face, as if he looked for any signs Relic might regret him. Finally, his expression turned intense. "I'll be right back." Stefan used his super speed to find Relic's lube and return. He was back before Relic barely knew he was gone. "Look into my eyes." The same swirling and mind-hazing sensation he had experienced last night overtook him again. This time, Stefan impaled him with his cock.

Relic moaned as the haze lifted from his mind.

"I didn't want to hurt you," Stefan admitted, explaining his reasoning for taking over Relic's mind. He kissed the corner of Relic's mouth. "It would kill me if I caused you harm."

Relic's body was on fire. He wanted a little harm. Relic writhed, trying to take what he wanted. Stefan kissed his way down Relic's chest. His fangs sank into a spot directly below Relic's collarbone. Relic cried out. He turned into the wildest power bottom alive. Relic clawed at Stefan's skin. He begged for more. Words flowed from him without meaning as he tried stealing Stefan's soul.

"Fuck me harder. I want it. The things I can do for you. You'll beg to stay here with me. Imagine what I could do while little too. I could climb inside your pants... holy shit." Stefan slammed forward, hitting the perfect spot. He didn't let up. Stefan fucked Relic exactly how he wanted. The edge got closer. Relic held his breath. His muscles tensed. He ground his back teeth. Then his soul sang as the ecstasy rocked him. He cried out, uncaring of the noises he made. Stefan's mouth covered his. He swallowed Relic's cries. Their tongues battled. Then Stefan threw his head back. The muscles in his neck strained.

"Relic. Goddamn."

Relic was mesmerized by the sight of Stefan's orgasm. When Stefan's chin lowered and his beautiful obsidian gaze met Relic's, Relic knew this was only the beginning. He would follow Stefan anywhere. There was something here.

As MUCH AS Stefan hated to get dressed and leave Relic's warm bed, the town needed its defenses fortified. Relic lived here. Stefan wouldn't risk him coming to harm. His stomach churned as he took to the sky, with Relic resting in his inner coat pocket. He didn't know what happened between them, but it felt powerful. Stefan couldn't pretend this had been only sex. He cared what happened to Relic. Stefan still couldn't believe he had betrayed his maker and told Relic the truth. It just wasn't in Stefan's heart to hurt this town, or the sprite who lived there. No doubt Magnus would kill him for this, or worse. There were so many things worse. He had to talk to Caspian.

The men worked where Stefan had left off that morning. Caspian glanced up, smiling before Stefan's feet hit the ground. Stefan thought he might be sick. Magnus had been in his head since the moment he opened his eyes, screaming for answers. Stefan had been ignoring him except for the occasional vague response while he focused on Relic. He couldn't avoid the truth forever. Magnus was desperate to have this place. He would strike soon. Stefan felt him moving closer by the second.

"We need to talk," Stefan said the moment he was on the ground.

Caspian flashed him a wry look. "We really don't."

Sometimes, Caspian confused him. "No. We really do. This place is in danger."

Caspian looked away and eyed the green grid that grew larger by the second. "The strangest thing happened to me last week," Caspian said, ignoring Stefan's warning. "Clara wanted a reading to know if she would ever have kids. I made my usual potion a little stronger than normal because I needed to take it sooner. While I waited for Clara to show up, I saw you. Just as clearly as I see you now, I saw you in Elvenwood. You were smiling in a way I'd never seen you smile before. So I looked closer, and do you know what else I saw?"

Stefan could barely breathe. He had never asked Caspian to look into his future before. He hadn't wanted to know how many years he would live enslaved to Magnus. But now, he had to know. "What did you see?"

Caspian swept open Stefan's jacket, revealing Relic hanging on every word. His gaze moved between them. "I saw the two of you mated."

Stefan's jaw slackened.

Caspian chuckled. "No one escapes fate or gets in her way. Magnus' plan won't work." Caspian walked away, whistling—like he hadn't floored Stefan.

Stefan dropped his gaze to Relic. Relic looked every bit as shellshocked as Stefan felt.

"Holy shit."

A smile slowly spread across Stefan's lips. "I knew you had me in knots for a reason. I just didn't know why."

Relic nodded, still looking wowed. "We need to get this wall finished. I can't risk losing you."

"So, this is why you've been ignoring me. You've just been standing around, lazy bastard."

Stefan's blood went cold at the sound of Magnus' voice. He pulled his jacket closed, hiding Relic from sight before turning to meet the dark, empty stare of his maker. Stefan didn't know if Magnus had been alive for so long that he had lost his humanity or if he had never had it. Either way, he had no soul and anyone looking at him could see it.

Another of Magnus' coven had Tafari held by the scruff while another had a knife held to a visibly outraged Hank's throat. Caspian's hands glowed green as he stayed ready to blast as soon as he had a clear shot. Stefan took in the scene before focusing on Magnus. He had to stay calm. Stefan couldn't let Relic's friends get hurt.

"I haven't been ignoring you."

Magnus snorted. "You know I hate liars." His expression turned cruel. "You also know I can reach into your head any time I like and get the truth."

A pain sliced through Stefan's skull, nearly taking him to his knees. He cried out in pain, trying to fight Magnus' intrusion.

"You can't fight, Stefan. Everything about you belongs to me. You've always been hardheaded, but you will obey. You will give me everything and then I'll take this town."

"I'll give you everything."

The pain disappeared as Relic's words cut through the haze.

Magnus turned to confront the human-sized Relic that appeared behind him. He wasn't quick enough.

"Including this stake," Relic added as he stabbed Magnus through the heart. The air stilled, and all sound died away as a moment passed where nothing happened. Magnus' gaze dropped to the wooden stake protruding from his chest. Stefan sprang forward, hoping to spare Relic from retribution. Magnus dropped as his legs turned to dust. The rest of him quickly followed before being carried away on the wind. His two cohorts stared in horror. Caspian took advantage of their distraction, blasting away the vampire who had held Hank. The moment Hank was free, he tore the head from the third vampire and tossed it aside. Stefan was frozen by his shock. He made a mental note not to fuck with Hank. Hank scooped up his wildcat and cradled him against his chest. As Stefan looked on, Tafari became a human, clinging to Hank. All of this was because of him. These were good men and they had been terrorized because of him.

Stefan met Relic's stare.

Relic closed the distance between them and cupped his face. "Stop. Don't do that. He was in control. You would never hurt anyone here."

Stefan couldn't breathe. Everyone would hate him after this. He wouldn't be allowed a home here with Relic.

With Tafari in his arms, Hank moved to Stefan's side. He slapped Stefan hard enough across the back to force him to finally fill his lungs with air. "Damn, boy. Snap out of it and take a breath. Your mate needs to know you're okay."

Stefan blinked. No one looked at him like this was his fault. In fact, everyone stared at him as if waiting to make sure he was okay. He blinked again. The world slowly came back into focus. He was free. Relic had freed him. He forced his lips to move.

"I thought you said you were just a little guy who would shrivel up like a juice box if I bit you."

A bark of laughter burst from Hank.

A sexy smile lit Relic's face. "Yeah, well. I also have a bit of a temper when it comes to the people I care about." He motioned toward his head. "It's the red hair."

Stefan took a step closer and snagged Relic's shirt. He hauled Relic into his arms and claimed his mouth. Stefan didn't care who watched. In the span of two hours, since he opened his eyes for the night, Relic had completely changed his life. While Stefan was still reeling from the knowledge he was free, he knew he had found his mate, his home, and his future. Stefan would never take a single moment of it for granted. Not a single one.

Chapter Twenty-One

PEOPLE DANCED, ate, and drank while Relic watched. He knew he could swell to human size and do the same. Instead, he stayed in Stefan's pocket, where he could hear the beat of Stefan's heart. It was a time for celebration, but Relic savored the knowledge he wasn't alone.

"It was nice of Clara to move her wedding to after sunset so I could come."

Relic nodded. "She's a nice person."

A sad-looking smile touched Stefan's lips. "Everyone here is nice."

"And everyone here loves you," Relic said, refusing to let Stefan fall back into the guilt that still plagued him occasionally.

Stefan's gaze dropped to Relic. "I love you."

Relic bit his bottom lip to keep from smiling like an idiot. Even though it wasn't the first time Stefan had said the words since he came to Elvenwood three months ago, Relic never tired of hearing them. "I love you too."

"We should do this too. Don't you think?"

Relic's mind slowed to a crawl. "Do what?"

Stefan motioned toward the crowd. "This. Get married."

A laugh sneaked out before Relic could stop it. "Not only are we mates, which is so much bigger than marriage, but we're also not human. Neither of us has the proper paperwork to secure a marriage license."

Stefan shrugged. "Still, we could do a handfasting or something like that. You could take my last name since sprites don't have one."

Relic turned the idea over in his mind. "Relic Chaucer. That has a certain ring to it."

"Oh. Speaking of nice rings." Stefan shifted positions and dug a small box from his pants pocket. "I have one for you, if you want it."

Relic zapped from Stefan's pocket to his knee, becoming big as he landed. "Are you serious? Did you really buy me a ring?"

Stefan nodded. "I won't steal any of Clara's thunder by getting on one knee, but I'll get on both knees later if you say yes."

"Absolutely, yes."

Stefan slipped the ring on Relic's finger and moved to steal a kiss. A loud gasp nearby brought their heads around. Clara covered her mouth and pointed at them. Guilt washed over Relic. He would never ruin anyone's wedding.

"Did you two just get engaged?"

Relic opened his mouth to apologize.

Clara didn't give him time. "At my wedding reception?"

"Clara, I'm—"

She rushed them and hugged them. "Oh, my god. I'm so honored. My love inspired your love. Caspian told me this would happen, but he didn't say who the couple would be. I can't believe it. I'm so glad it was you. That means Stefan is staying and we have our very own vampire in Elvenwood. This is just so amazing; I feel so blessed to be the one who spread love."

Relic didn't know how much of that was technically true, but he was too relieved Clara wasn't upset to care. "Thank you."

She kissed his cheek. "Of course. I have to get back to my hubby."

They all looked Scott's way. The man looked like the most besotted fool on the planet. He was a bit plain, to be honest, and likely he wouldn't normally catch a single eye, but he obviously adored Clara.

"Yes. He does look lost without you," Stefan said, forcing Relic to turn his head to hide his smile. Scott really did. That was what made Stefan's droll tone twice as funny.

The moment they were alone, Relic buried his face against Stefan's throat and shook with laughter. He was too happy to contain it. Their little town of Elvenwood was safe and Relic had found the man of his dreams. Eternity looked damn good from where he sat on Stefan's lap. Nothing but bright skies were ahead of them from here.

Introduction to Witchin Yuletide

Elvenwood has a new citizen, and he has a big… personality. Thankfully, there's a vet in town who can handle him.

On his way home from ice fishing, Miles finds a bear caught in a trap. He thinks the poor animal is dead until it turns into a man and pleads for his help. Nursing Poe back to health might be a huge responsibility, but Miles is up for the challenge. Hopefully, Miles is also up for the rest of what Poe has to offer.

Witchin Yuletide is the sixth book in Charity Parkerson's Witchin series. These fun, short paranormal romances are meant to be devoured on your lunch break. Read along as a tiny town in Ohio grows its supernatural community one resident at a time.

Chapter Twenty-Two

SNOW CRUNCHED BENEATH MILES' boots. When he was a kid, he had loved this time of year. As an adult, not so much. The tip of his nose was frozen, and his fingers had gone numb an hour ago. Plus, he hadn't caught a damn thing during his ice-fishing trip, but the silence had been golden. As a single man with no kids, his life should be quiet as hell. But Miles had chosen to be a veterinarian and now he listened to dogs bark all day. It was a good thing he loved dogs. Miles ran his fingers through Sonny's fur in an apology for his thoughts. He had no complaints about his life. Miles just enjoyed the quiet more nowadays than he ever expected. And Christmas was right around the corner, which always reminded him of how empty his life was these days.

With his tackle box and poles in hand, Miles trekked through the snow, weaving through the trees on the way back to his truck. "No fish for dinner tonight. Guess I'll have to pull something from the freezer to defrost."

Sonny barked and ran ahead.

Miles kept his head down against the wind. Sonny ran back to him, circled him, barking, and then ran off again. This time, Sonny's actions caught his attention. They had been out in the cold too long for even a Siberian husky to still have this much energy. Miles followed the dog. A huge, dark lump came into view. Sonny ran around it, barking before darting back to Miles.

Miles set his stuff down and patted the dog. "God boy. What did you find?" Miles moved closer. He realized too late it was a bear. It was curled into a ball and had snow covering its fur, making it harder for Miles to recognize it as an animal until he was too close for his comfort. Miles froze. Fuck. He had not intended to get eaten by a bear today. Sonny tried to move back to the animal's side. Miles grabbed his collar and held on. He took a step back, pulling Sonny along with him. "Shhh. Let's just back away slowly."

The bear moved.

Miles froze.

Its head lifted.

Miles turned to run. He could come back for his stuff later if he lived.

"Help."

The plea stopped Miles in his tracks. He glanced back. Where the bear had once been, a man was in its place. He was naked and blood flowed from his leg. In the back of his mind, Miles recognized he was dealing with a Werebear. After all, the Were population had been growing in Elvenwood for the past year or so. But all Miles saw was a man in need, and he had to help. He rushed forward.

"What happened?" It was a dumbass question. There was a bear trap connected to the man's leg. Miles' head was just a panicked mess, and the question was the first thing to pop to his lips. He shook his head at his own ridiculousness. "Don't answer that. What's your name?"

He inspected the trap and the injuries. Miles needed to get the man to his office. If he released the trap now, he might cause the man to bleed out, but he didn't know if he could move the guy alone. Miles needed to get him talking and stave off shock for as long as possible.

"Poe."

The weak-sounding answer came out on a gasp as the man lost consciousness. Miles' panic doubled. They were out in the middle of the woods. Poe was a Were and three times Miles' size. He couldn't call an ambulance and he didn't have any medical supplies. Miles whipped out his phone and called the first place that popped into his head.

"Future's Untold. Caspian speaking."

Miles thanked every deity listening for the quick answer. "Caspian. It's Dr. Brown. I found a Were-bear in the woods. He has a bear trap on his leg, and I didn't know who else to call."

Thankfully, Caspian stayed calmer than Miles. "Put me on speakerphone."

Miles did as told. "Okay."

"Use your phone to capture your location, then text it to 555-8967. Got it?"

Miles nodded along as he followed Caspian's instructions. "Done."

"I'll be there shortly. Just hang tight."

Miles disconnected the call without saying goodbye. His focus was locked on his patient. Miles eyed the man's nude body. He was turning blue. After a quick check of Poe's pulse, Miles stood and peeled off his coat. Poe needed it more than him. Without thinking, Miles' gaze wandered. Poe was huge. His muscles were thick and his chest wide. The guy's cock was massive. Miles felt a bit guilty for noticing, but really, there was no avoiding it. Poe's dick was right there, and truly, Miles had never seen one so big. It was like Poe had become a man, but his dick hadn't. Miles quickly tossed his coat over Poe. He had to stop looking. For fuck's sake. Poe was bleeding everywhere, and Miles was eye-fucking the poor guy. Miles had no idea what had gotten into him.

Thankfully, Caspian was there in no time, saving Miles from himself. Caspian had his husband Brock with him and one of the local policemen, Wade, who was married to a Werewolf. Caspian motioned the men's way. "I brought help since I didn't know what to expect."

Miles nodded. He was cold as fuck. Help seemed like a good way to make things faster. "Good. I'm betting he's pretty damn heavy."

Caspian eyed Poe for a moment, assessing his injuries. He stopped and touched the trap. Caspian immediately drew his hand back. "Goddamn it. It's cursed. We need to get him somewhere warm so I can take a closer look." He met Miles' stare. "Can we use your cabin? You're the closest."

Miles didn't hesitate. "Of course. We need to bind his leg before we lift him."

Caspian straightened. "Don't worry. I have this." He snapped his fingers, and a green light filled his hand. Poe's body lifted along with the trap. He was completely stiff, as if Caspian's magic bound him. Miles had known Caspian was a warlock and powerful. That was why Miles had called him, but Miles had never seen Caspian in action. It was impressive.

The coat almost slipped from Poe's body. Miles caught it and made sure Poe stayed covered.

Caspian looked Brock's way. "Will you open the back of the SUV so we can get him inside?"

Brock nodded and rushed ahead.

Caspian looked Wade's way. "Do you mind using your sirens to get us there quickly?"

"No problem," Wade said. He followed in Brock's wake.

Poe's body floated through the air. Miles followed. He fought the urge to dance in place with a need to help. Miles felt useless. He wanted to treat those injuries, but he couldn't yet. It was maddening.

As if Caspian felt his desperation, he nodded toward the waiting vehicles. "You should be the first car behind Wade. That way, you can get inside and start gathering whatever medical supplies you need. I can break the curse on this trap, but the wound might not immediately heal the way most Were wounds do. Someone meant to hurt him, and they succeeded. They won't have made it easy for him to recover."

Caspian's claim had Miles' heart twisting. He loved animals. The idea of anyone intentionally hurting one was a hot button for him. He had to do something.

With a nod, Miles rushed ahead and yanked open his truck door. As soon as Sonny was inside, Miles tossed his fishing gear in the back and jumped behind the wheel. His impatience was through the roof as he waited for Wade to pull out, sirens blaring. Miles immediately pulled out behind him. He watched in his mirror as Brock's SUV filed in behind them. They couldn't get to Miles' place fast enough. Miles kept thinking about Poe's skin turning blue. He needed to get Poe warm and settled. The idea that someone had purposely done this kept bombarding his brain. Miles wanted to punch some-one. There was nothing he hated more than people who abused animals.

As they pulled into the driveway of Miles' two-story cabin, he practically leaped from the truck. Sonny followed on his heels and then darted around him to get to the door first. Miles unlocked the front door and shooed the rest of his dogs into the bathroom before shutting them inside. With no fear of his pets being under anyone's feet, Miles headed for the bedroom. He pulled back the covers and then threw towels down so he could freshen the bed once Poe's wounds were dressed.

Poe's body floated into the room, with Caspian at the helm. The moment he was on the bed, Caspian went to work on the trap while Miles waited for his cue to treat the wound. The trap snapped open, and Caspian tossed it aside. His hands glowed green again as he tried sealing the wounds.

"Fuck." The growled curse didn't give Miles hope.

Miles glanced at Brock and Wade. Their expressions matched his thoughts. Something wasn't right.

"I can stop the bleeding and set the break, but I can't heal him completely. He'll have to recover naturally. Whoever cursed that trap made certain he couldn't use magic to heal."

Miles wasn't worried about that part. As long as Poe would heal eventually, Miles could handle the rest. "I can take care of him. Just do what you can."

Caspian met his stare. "He's no danger to you."

Miles nodded. "I'm not even thinking about that. He needs help and I can give it."

With a nod, Caspian went back to working on Poe's leg. Finally, he stood. "I've done all I can do. It's on you now, doc."

Miles didn't hesitate. He jumped in to take over. He swabbed Poe's leg and bound it. He would wait for a cast until some of the swelling subsided. With the leg cleaned and bandaged, Miles swept the dirty towels from the bed and removed his coat. He stepped back to discard everything, and everyone moved closer to the bed.

"Holy shit." Wade's whispered curse caught Miles' attention.

Before he could ask a single question, Caspian chimed in, "You're all looking at the same thing I am, right? Like I'm not just being a perv."

Brock shook his head. "It's not just you. Jesus Christ. That thing is massive."

"I can't look away," Wade said, sounding horrified. "I've never seen a dong that fucking big."

Miles grabbed the covers and pulled them over Poe's body. He didn't know why he felt a little possessive, but he did. Miles told himself he was just being protective of his patient. It didn't feel that way.

Brock and Wade cleared their throats and visibly tried looking everywhere but at each other.

Caspian squeezed Miles' shoulder. He looked mildly shellshocked. "Um, I'm not sure if I envy you or pity you, but good luck."

Miles had no idea what that meant. "Okay." Poe was just a patient, but Miles didn't point that out. Miles didn't know why he couldn't say the words. His gaze slid back Poe's way. Without thinking, he stroked Poe's long hair. Miles would take care of him. No one else would harm him. Poe was right where he belonged. Miles shook his head at the thought. Poe was in the best place to get care. That was what Miles meant. Miles wasn't being creepy. He just cared. Nothing else.

Two SETS of sweet brown eyes and a set of light blue ones stared at Poe while panting. He eyed the dogs. None of them looked familiar. His gaze moved around the room. A fire crackled in a nearby fireplace. Through an open door, he caught sight of a Christmas tree. The bed he currently occupied actually fit his large body. Still, nothing looked familiar. His leg hurt like the fires of hell had it in its grasp. He pulled the thick comforter aside and stared down at his body. A cast covered his leg from below the knee to above his toes. The memory of a bear trap snapping closed on his leg assailed him. Poe dropped his head back onto the pillow. That was one nightmare he hoped not to repeat.

The blue-eyed husky trotted from the room. In a matter of seconds, he returned with the most beautiful man Poe had ever set eyes on. He smiled when he saw Poe awake.

"Hey. I was beginning to wonder if you would ever wake up, but I also worried you'd be in pain when you did. How are you feeling?"

"Confused," Poe said, answering honestly.

The guy pushed the blanket aside enough to check Poe's leg. He pressed on Poe's toes and knee. "Your circulation still looks good. Do you need anything for the pain?"

Poe shook his head. "Who are you?"

A sweet smile touched the man's lips. "Sorry. You've been here a few days. I guess I've become so accustomed to seeing you I forgot you don't know me. I'm Dr. Brown. The veterinarian for these parts. You can call me Miles."

"How did I get here?"

Miles sat on the edge of the bed and felt of Poe's forehead. He smelled fucking amazing. "I was ice fishing when I found you caught in a trap. Some friends of mine came and helped me bring you here. I didn't figure you'd want me to drop you at a hospital, considering your species. While I don't know much about Weres, animals are still my specialty. I can take care of you."

Pie blinked. "You know about Weres?"

A smile exploded across Miles' lips. "Sir, this is Elvenwood. We pride ourselves on our diverse supernatural community."

His mind raced. "This is Elvenwood?" His muscles relaxed. "So I made it." Poe's eyes fell closed.

Miles rubbed his arm. "What do you need? Are you hungry? Thirsty? Can I call someone for you?"

Poe shook his head and opened his eyes again. "There's no one."

The kindness in Miles' eyes held him captivated. "Do you need me to help you to the bathroom?"

Poe forced himself to sit up. His head spun.

Miles was right there, supporting him. "Don't move too fast. You lost a lot of blood and you've been out for three days. You haven't had any fluids beyond an IV."

"I don't understand why I feel so bad. People like me heal almost immediately. I should've been on my feet as soon as I was freed from that trap."

Miles rubbed his back. Poe wasn't sure Miles was even conscious of the way he touched Poe. "Our local warlock says it was a cursed trap. You'll heal, but it'll be more in line with the way a human heals."

Damn. He should have known that shady mother-fucker Sean would curse him every way he could. That was why he had been headed for Elvenwood when he found out Sean had cheated. Elvenwood was supposed to be a haven for people like him. He had known, even though Sean was at fault, Sean wouldn't let him go without a fight. Even while fucking everyone else, Sean had been controlling and possessive. Having a crazy ex was one thing. Having a crazy ex who was also a warlock was another. For some dumbass reason, he hadn't expected Sean to physically hurt him, though. That was a new level of bullshit. Poe was glad they were done. It had been a long time coming.

When Poe caught his breath, he took another look around the room. There was a bathroom about six feet from the bed. He was pretty sure he could make it with help. The three dogs blocked the path.

"Who are your friends?"

Miles looked the dogs' way. He pointed at the husky. "Sonny." Then the beagle. "Cher." Then a mixed breed that looked to be part boxer. "Elvis."

Poe scooted to the edge of the bed and forced his legs over the side. The small act had him out of breath again. He kept up his end of the conversation to distract himself. "Music lover?"

A sexy laugh caressed Poe's ears as Miles moved to help him stand. "An animal lover who's running out of names."

Poe stood. His head spun again. He ground his back teeth.

"Lean on me."

"I'll crush you." Poe forced the words out through clenched teeth. He had never felt so much pain at once. Poe hated being weak.

Gorgeous blue eyes focused on him. "You won't."

Poe couldn't look away. Miles took the lead and Poe followed, hobbling his way to the bathroom. Miles didn't let him fall. Once inside the bathroom, Poe clung to the vanity. He caught sight of himself in the mirror. Poe expected he would look like hell, but he didn't. His hair had been recently brushed. His beard looked freshly trimmed. It seemed Miles had been taking amazing care of him.

He washed his face and took the world's longest piss. Bears reused their fluids during hibernation but when they woke up, damn. Afterward, he washed his hands, trying to feel halfway human again. It wasn't until Poe opened the bathroom door and found Miles waiting that it really hit him. He was nude. At heart, he was an animal. Clothes didn't matter that much to him. Miles was human, yet he also didn't bat an eye.

"Let's get you back to bed and I'll make you something to eat."

"Whatever the doc says," Poe quipped, trying to hide his exhaustion as Miles helped him back into bed. This healing like a human was some bullshit. He didn't like it at all.

Once he was settled, sitting up and leaned against a stack of pillows, Miles squeezed his shoulder. "I'll be right back."

Poe snagged his hand before he could get away. "Thank you."

Miles held his stare. "Of course. You're safe here."

Poe didn't release Miles right away. His thumb brushed Miles' wrist. Miles' lips parted in surprise. Poe swore a spark shot up his arm. Miles startled, as if he felt it too. The truth hit Poe, and he immediately dropped Miles' hand. It couldn't be. He had just left one relationship, and he had purposely steered clear of any chances of accidentally finding his true mate over the years. Yet here he was. Poe had never expected it to be so obvious. He had always thought it might be a slow revelation like it had been with his parents. This guy was human. There was just no way.

"I should call someone to get me, and get out of your hair."

A deep line appeared between Miles' eyebrows. "Absolutely not. You're not going anywhere until I give the okay. Do you understand?"

Poe swore Miles got bigger with each outraged word. An unexpected smile slowly spread across Poe's lips. "Yes, sir."

Miles gave him a sharp nod and stormed off while Poe watched his ass for every step. Maybe this human could handle him after all. Poe was willing to stick around and find out.

Chapter Twenty-Three

It took Poe three days to feel halfway normal again. No matter how hard he argued to move to the couch and get out of Miles' bed, Miles wouldn't budge. It was more than just feeling like an inconvenience. The sheets smelled like Miles. Scents were his weakness. It was driving him wild. He had tons of time to think. Miles knew about the supernaturals living amongst humans, but Poe didn't know if Miles understood mates. He doubted anyone had prepared him to be tied for life to a bear. Poe would leave when he healed enough to go. Miles had been nothing but kind to him. Poe couldn't disrupt his life.

Miles came through the bedroom door all smiles, carrying crutches in one hand and a bag of food in the other. "Hey. Look what I finally found. Crutches big enough for you," he said, shaking them at Poe. "The pharmacist knows a guy who had these lying around. He let me borrow them." Miles held the crutches out to Poe. "Give them a go."

Poe tossed the covers aside, thankful Miles had found him a pair of pajama shorts that fit. He flashed Miles a grateful smile as he accepted the crutches. His stomach growled at the scent wafting from the bag Miles held.

"Is that burgers you're holding?"

Miles bit his bottom lip and backed toward the door. "You'll have to come find me to see." He walked away, leaving Poe with the crutches and a hunger for more than charred beef.

Poe eyed the set of aluminum sticks. They didn't look sturdy enough to hold his weight. He imagined normal people never thought about weight restrictions. It was all someone like him thought about when trying new things. He used the crutches to brace himself enough to stand. When they held up through that, he shoved them beneath his arms and took a tentative hop. They didn't bend. Poe did it again. A sigh of relief rang through his mind as he hobbled from the room without destroying his new tools. His first real glimpse of the living room stopped him in his tracks. The place was beautiful. It was obviously a log cabin, but it was more like a lodge than a home. The place was huge. The upstairs could be seen from downstairs. He eyed the wooden landing above him, trying to see what Miles kept upstairs. It looked like a pool table. He couldn't see the rest. Another fire crackled in a fireplace inside the living room. Stockings hung from the mantel. One for each dog. He didn't see one for Miles. The Christmas tree looked like something out of a magazine. It was decorated to perfection.

Poe hopped past the leather couch and followed his nose to find Miles. He found him inside a large kitchen with two stoves and more cabinets than Poe had ever seen in his life.

"I guess being a vet pays pretty well."

Miles glanced over his shoulder and smiled. "What do you do?"

Poe made his way to the oak kitchen table and sat. The short trip had worn him out. "I used to work at the mill in Clovertown. They laid me off a month ago. I haven't really had much luck finding work since then."

Miles carried a plate to the table and set it in front of Poe. Three hamburgers and a large helping of fries piled the plate. Poe's mouth watered. Miles walked away and came back with iced tea. "I imagine not," Miles said, as if serving Poe was second nature and meant nothing. "We have two Weres in town and neither have any real identity that'll hold up under scrutiny. It doesn't matter here in Elvenwood, but I'm sure it would matter greatly to the IRS."

Poe snagged Miles' arm before he could get away again. "Thank you for everything you've done for me. Anyone else probably would've killed me the second they saw me."

A wry smile touched Miles' lips. "You don't have to keep thanking me. I'm just glad I found you when I did." Miles pulled away and moved back to the counter to grab his plate and glass before returning to Poe's side. He pulled out the closest chair and sat. Poe moved his chair even closer on the sly, wanting to feel the heat from Miles' skin. Miles took a bite from his burger and swallowed before speaking again. "The other day, you said you'd made it when I mentioned you were in Elvenwood. What had you headed our way?"

Poe took a huge bite of his hamburger to buy himself time.

Miles didn't let it slide. "Does it have anything to do with someone attacking you with a cursed bear trap?"

Poe's mind raced as he chewed. Ultimately, he knew he needed to be honest. He swallowed. "My ex-boyfriend is a warlock. I caught him in our bed with someone else and I stormed out. He's pretty unstable, so I knew he would likely try something, but I didn't know what. My cousin told me about Elvenwood a while back. He said people with bad intentions can't find this place, so I headed this way, hoping I'd make it before Sean snapped. I didn't make it," Poe added unnecessarily. He took another bite to keep from checking Miles' reaction.

For several minutes, Miles didn't speak. When he finally did, he sounded hesitant. "That's pretty much exactly how I ended up in Elvenwood."

Poe looked Miles' way. "Your ex is a crazy warlock?"

An adorable-sounding snort escaped Miles. The way he curled his nose made Poe want to smooth away the wrinkles just to feel how soft Miles' pale skin was. His blond hair looked velvety too. Really, all of him looked squishy and huggable. Poe really wanted to touch him.

"No. My ex-husband was a mean drunk. We went to high school together. He played football while I was just the nerdy kid. I guess I thought I should be lucky someone like him even looked at someone like me, so I put up with more than I should. After I got my degree, I started my own practice and he sort of settled into being a stay-at-home husband. But really, he drank all day, fucked anything with a pulse, and hit me if I disagreed with his ways."

Poe had a rage growing in his gut that had nowhere to go.

Miles kept talking, oblivious to Poe's dangerous crawl toward shifting. "Anyhow, I came home one day to find him three sheets to the wind with two naked men in the hot tub I paid for, and I lost it. And then he lost it and I jumped in my car and drove until I couldn't stand the pain of my broken arm any longer. It turned out this town needed a vet, and I needed a new start. So I got an order of protection, used the police reports and doctor reports to divorce him without being stuck paying alimony, and stayed here." Miles shrugged. "Now it's just my dogs and me." He ate a fry like his story meant nothing.

Poe fought his claws from bursting from his hands. He doubted his cast, or his leg, would handle the shift. Poe breathed through his nose. "That won't happen to you again." Poe's voice sounded as deadly as he felt. The bear inside him wanted to protect its mate.

Miles smiled. There wasn't an ounce of happiness in the gesture. "I doubt I'll ever find anyone again, so you're right." Miles stood, even though he was nowhere near finished with his food. "You should eat. You're still regaining your strength." It was obvious he wanted to run before Poe saw any of his insecurities.

"Can you hear me when I speak to you like this?"

Miles' gaze shot to Poe's as the words obviously penetrated his mind.

"How did you do that?"

Poe smiled. "If you're running away, go ask your friend Caspian what that means." Poe took a bite of his burger. Satisfaction stole his temper. Miles would run and he would ask. Now the ball was in Miles' court. Just as Miles had ended up in this town for a reason, so had Poe. No one escaped fate. It looked like he would be staying after all. Miles had his attention and Poe never backed down from a challenge.

As MUCH AS Miles didn't want to look like a coward, he was curious as hell, and Poe had seen too much of Miles' insecurities. He had heard Poe's voice in his head. Miles had to know why. If Poe didn't intend to tell him, Miles had to do what Poe said. He had to find Caspian. He took his food with him and didn't look back. Miles ate as he drove. First, he tried Future's Untold, the psychic shop Caspian owned. When he found the place closed, Miles headed to Caspian's place. Caspian opened the door before

Miles knocked, as if he had been expected. He waved Miles inside.

Miles unwound his scarf as he stepped through the door. "I guess you know why I'm here."

Caspian's sweet brown eyes flashed with humor. "Yeah. So don't freak out, okay?"

Miles sat on the first empty seat he came to, the recliner. "If I didn't freak out when I brought a bear to stay in my home, I'm not about to start now." Miles liked to think he was a calm person. He had seen a lot of wild things in Elvenwood. It would take a lot to scare him.

Caspian didn't sit. He eyed Miles with heavy skepticism, etching his features. "Are you sure? Because sometimes I really do see the future and I saw this moment. You were nowhere near as calm as you're about to try to convince me."

"I'm perfectly fine," Miles said, adding an eye roll for effect. He couldn't let anyone see him as weak. "It sounds like you're the only one trying to be convincing."

Caspian nodded. "Okay. Poe is your mate."

Miles blinked. "Yeah. I don't know what that means."

Finally, Caspian moved to the couch and sat. "It means Poe was born carrying a sliver of your soul and you were born with part of his. You were meant to find each other and spend the rest of your lives together."

Miles did his best to keep his nerves under control. "So you mean soulmates."

"Sort of," Caspian said, sounding patient. "Except you both have magic in your blood. Your lives are tied together. He can project his thoughts to you, and you can do the same. You can choose to live your lives apart, but really, you can't because you'd miss each other every day until you both died of a very, very old age."

It was getting harder by the second to be calm. "How very?"

"Hundreds of years. Probably longer."

Miles sucked in a breath. He stood. Any second, he would completely lose his shit and Miles did not do those type things when people were watching. His ex had taught him one important lesson: never show weakness. "Thank you for telling me. I'll consider everything you've said."

Caspian smiled like he knew something Miles didn't, which was probably everything. Miles couldn't think about that, though. He had too much in his head. "Be careful going home."

Miles nodded and headed back out to his truck. He backed from the driveway and drove aimlessly around town before ending up at a department store. It wasn't a big place like the one three towns over, but Miles just needed a place to wander while he thought.

He grabbed a shopping cart and lost himself in his thoughts. His feet carried him to the men's section. Miles picked out some clothes for Poe while he shied away from everything Caspian said. Over the years, men and women had asked Miles on dates. He had always shut them down. Not only did he think no one really wanted him, he was scared to love someone else who did nothing but hurt him. Poe was a huge guy. He could easily crush Miles physically. It was his heart he feared for the most, though. That organ had been through so much. He didn't think it could handle another betrayal.

Poe was gorgeous. Miles didn't doubt he turned heads everywhere he went. Goosebumps rose on Miles' skin just thinking about Poe touching him. He blinked away the images in his head. Miles found himself standing in the Christmas aisle. Wrapping paper and gift bags lined the shelves. Longing struck from nowhere. Miles wanted a real life. A full life with laughter and love. He didn't know Poe, but he was a lot more smitten than he cared to admit. Poe watched him with a possessiveness Miles had never experienced. Miles had caught Poe sniffing his skin when Poe thought he wasn't looking. Most of all, Miles felt less alone than he ever had since Poe came into his life. While Miles still didn't know what he wanted or expected, he cared. That counted for something.

Miles grabbed rolls of wrapping paper, tape, and bows before shifting gears. He fell into shopping mode. Maybe he didn't know much, but he knew Christmas was right around the corner. Poe wouldn't be well enough to leave before then. He might not know where they were headed, but he knew he wouldn't be alone this year, and neither would Poe.

Miles found a nice bottle of cologne and a Sherpa-lined jacket that would look great against Poe's skin. Gift after gift filled his cart. He would stop by his office and wrap them before heading home. Maybe he didn't know what mates were, how they acted, or what they did, but he knew he was happy for the first time in a long time. That counted for something to him. Poe meant something.

Chapter Twenty-Four

WITH HIS LEG resting on the coffee table, Poe stared into the fire and chewed the side of his nail. It had been hours since Miles ran for his life without a word. A small part of Poe wished he had never said anything. He should have left well enough alone. But Miles had been sitting so close, smelling delicious, yet sounding so sad. Poe hadn't been able to take it. There was a kindness in Miles that Poe hadn't seen in years. It was addictive. Still, the way Miles had stayed gone said a lot. A life with Poe wasn't what he wanted. That was fair. Poe was just a bear with no job. Miles didn't know him. Hell, he was practically a stranger. Miles had found him in a cursed bear trap, for fuck's sake. He really couldn't expect Miles to be the least bit interested. But damn, Poe really wanted him to be interested.

The front door opened, sending the dogs running toward the cold that blasted inside. "I know. I know. Damn. Let me get through the door."

Poe watched Miles struggle his way inside, pulling a collapsible wagon filled with brightly wrapped gifts. He wanted to rush and help, but he still wasn't rushing anywhere.

"What's all this?"

Miles glanced up from the dogs attacking his feet. His smile was bright, and the tip of his nose was red. He looked sexy as hell. "Hey. I went shopping." He dragged the wagon to the tree and left it. "It's Christmas in a few days and we should have a proper one, don't you think?"

Poe's gaze moved to the pile of gifts. "I hope you don't mean those are for me."

Miles' smile faltered. "Why? Is that a problem?"

Discomfort crawled up Poe's neck. "Well, I mean, I'm stuck here with no way to get you anything. That's not fair."

Miles shrugged. "If I want something, I'll buy it, but I don't really need anything. Plus, it's a huge gift not to be alone. It's usually just the dogs and me. That's super depressing. So if you want to get me something, then agree to enjoy the holiday with me. No regrets."

Even though Poe still hated the idea of not giving Miles anything, he nodded. "Okay. If that's what you want."

A smile exploded across Miles' face. "Yay. Now, do you need anything? Would you like some hot chocolate?"

"I'd like for you to sit still. Just stay put and keep me company."

Miles unwound his scarf and tossed it aside. "Okay." He unzipped his jacket and peeled it off before draping it over the arm of the couch.

Poe didn't give him time to get settled. "Did you talk to Caspian?"

"*I did.*"

A ridiculous smile tugged at Poe's lips as the words brushed across his mind. He hadn't realized how much he would like the sensation. Still, just because Miles talked to Caspian, and had spoken to him mentally, didn't mean this was something he wanted. "I'm sorry you were thrust into this. Trust me, I totally get that I'm a stranger. You deserved some warning, so don't worry. I won't rush you or anything."

Miles' expression went through a myriad of emotions while Poe rambled before landing on hurt.

It hit Poe. Miles didn't think Poe wanted him. He thought Poe felt obligated, or possibly trapped, and Poe's talk of not rushing obviously cemented that fear in Miles' mind. Of course, it wasn't true at all. Mates were everything in his world and he had gotten the most beautiful one of all. He didn't know how to explain any of that to Miles without making things worse, so he kept rambling. "You're absolutely gorgeous and I get that I'm just like this big lump. If you want me to leave when I'm better and never look back, I understand. You could do way better than a bear with no job, but I'm thrilled you're meant for me. Hell, I feel like the luckiest—"

Miles shot forward and kissed Poe. It was just a quick press of lips on lips, but it stopped the nervous flow of words pouring from Poe. Miles smiled. "You're wanted." He swept a heated look down Poe's body, setting Poe's skin ablaze. "So fucking wanted."

Heat climbed Poe's cheeks. The blush hit him from nowhere. "Really?"

Desire poured from Miles. Poe could smell the change in the air. Miles nodded. His intense gaze made it harder for Poe to catch his breath. "I won't rush you, though."

Poe blinked. He didn't understand how the tables had turned.

Miles' wicked expression had Poe's body stirring. Miles kept talking, making things worse. "This whole mate thing might be unexpected and new to me, but I wanted you before any of that came to light. I've thought about you... us... together, a lot, to be honest. I've berated myself over it, since you're my patient. But I can't help myself and I should be quiet now. You're blushing like I'm horrifying you. Sorry. I'm not very good at this."

"I think you're amazing." The confession popped out without thinking too much about it. Poe just spoke from the heart. "From the moment I opened my eyes and saw you, I've been addicted to seeing you again. I have to force myself not to touch you, but I want to."

Poe swore Miles didn't blink as he held Poe's stare. "Where do you want to touch me?"

Poe's tongue shot out, wetting his bottom lip. He swore he could already taste Miles. "Everywhere. I want to feel your weight straddling my hips." His gaze dropped to Miles' mouth. "I want to taste your tongue."

Miles moved. He was slow at first, as if he expected Poe's rejection. His palm landed on Poe's bare shoulder as he shifted potions. Poe had to fight to keep his eyes open at the sensation of skin on skin. It was his mate touching him. His. The possessiveness was bigger than anything he ever faced. Then Miles carefully straddled Poe's lap, visibly being extra cautious of Poe's injuries. Poe didn't give a fuck about his leg. He couldn't feel anything below his dick.

"You should take your shirt off so I can feel your skin against mine." The growl in Poe's voice was more bear than human. It was out of his control.

Miles took off his shirt.

Poe still didn't look away from the beautiful blue eyes holding his stare. He flattened his hand against Miles' back and drew him closer. Miles braced his palms against the couch on either side of Poe's head. Poe lost his patience and closed the gap between them, capturing Miles' lips. They opened at the same time, as if equally desperate to taste each other. Their tongues brushed. Poe's cock jumped like it had been licked. The desire to have Miles in every way was so intense, Poe thought his mind would snap. No one had warned him it would be like this. His parents had told him he would ache without his mate once they found each other. Poe hadn't known they meant like this. He hurt from the need for more. Their kiss was animalistic. Almost violent. They fought to get closer. Poe knew there was no way Miles didn't feel the hard cock pulsing to be inside him.

"I'm not rushing you," Poe said as he changed directions and reclaimed Miles' mouth.

Miles' hand moved between their bodies. He massaged Poe's cock through his thin shorts. A ragged gasp tore from Poe. He ripped his mouth away and pressed his forehead to Miles' shoulder as he fought for air. Miles didn't stop torturing him. His fingers found their way inside Poe's shorts while Poe watched.

"Oh, God. You're killing me."

An evil-sounding chuckle brushed Poe's ear at his confession. "I want this inside me."

Poe fought to breathe and think at the same time. "Um." He licked his lips. Poe had never felt more parched. "We're going to need all the lube. People don't find sex with me to be particularly pleasant." He hated talking about this. "That's why my ex was always cheating. He said it hurt too much to be with me."

Miles kissed the shell of his ear. "I'm not afraid. You should see the size of some of my toys. Your package feels perfect to me." He emphasized his claim by squeezing Poe's cock. Poe didn't know how much more he could take. Then Miles was gone. He slipped from Poe's lap and headed for the bedroom. Poe stayed put, blinking like an idiot. He didn't know if he was supposed to follow. Then a very nude Miles returned with lube in hand. His beautiful body held Poe captivated as Miles crossed the room. He was blonde everywhere. Miles was hard, and Poe's mouth watered. That cock was his. Poe would suck it.

Miles straddled his lap again. Poe sat helplessly as Miles worked Poe's shorts down just far enough to set his erection free. Miles kept his head bowed and his gaze fixed on thoroughly lubing Poe's erection. Poe couldn't look away from Miles. He silently begged for Miles to lift his chin and meet his stare. Poe wanted to see his eyes. He needed to know if this was what Miles truly wanted.

"*Look at me.*"

Miles' chin lifted at the mental plea. His eyes were soft and filled with emotions that only a true mate would understand. Poe still needed Miles to grasp the magnitude of the moment. "If we do this, you'll never want anyone else. You'll be stuck with me."

Miles tossed the lube aside and moved closer. His arms encircled Poe's neck. "I already don't want anyone else. What about you?"

Poe wrapped his arm around Miles' waist and easily lifted him, leaving Miles no other choice than to get his feet beneath him, squatting over Poe's erection. He used his free hand to position his cock against Miles' asshole. Poe never looked away from holding Miles' stare. "No one else exists anymore."

Miles pressed down, taking Poe's crown. His head fell back as he visibly fought for air as he slowly sank down, taking all of Poe.

Poe could barely breathe. Not only did no one enjoy sex with him, no one had ever taken all of him. Miles made sounds like he was in heaven. His chin lowered. Heat blasted Poe from the lust written in every line of Miles' face.

"Fuck me."

At Miles' growled demand, Poe pulled Miles' face to his and bit his bottom lip. Miles came back at him every bit as hard, licking and biting. Poe pushed with his good foot, lifting his hips and trying to get deeper. Miles bounced on Poe's dick, taking what he wanted. It was violent. They weren't making love. It was a claiming. Poe marked his territory. Miles stole his soul. Poe's scalp stung from Miles pulling his hair. He gasped and moaned against Poe's lips and around his tongue. Reality disappeared. There was nothing but the pleasure. Miles' nails scored Poe's skin. His teeth sank into Poe's bottom lip and held on as cries vibrated from him. Hot cum hit Poe's chest, taking him by surprise. Then Miles' body violently sucked him deeper as a spasm shook Miles' entire body. Poe gasped and squeezed his eyes shut. The pressure climbing his shaft exploded into a soul-rocking orgasm. He lost all sense of sight and sound as waves of pleasure shook him. Poe pumped Miles' ass full of cum. He knew his sexy mate would leak for hours. Possessiveness caused a growl to vibrate from his throat at just the thought. This man was his. *His.* Poe would kill anyone who dared to touch him. His body tried to shift with only the idea of anyone else ever having this with Miles. He fought against it.

Poe forced his eyes open. He needed to focus on the man on his cock if he hoped to stay human.

Miles held his face cradled between his hands. His blue eyes were soft. Poe's rage slipped away, and the truth settled in his chest. He had never loved anyone before now. Poe's pride had been hurt by Sean's bull-shit, but Poe hadn't known this. Miles was the person chosen for him by a power bigger than them. They had never stood a chance of escaping this, and Poe was more grateful than he could ever say.

"I think it would kill me if you left."

Miles' confession made Poe's eyes burn. "I think I'd die if I tried."

There was nothing more to say, really. They belonged together. It was inescapable.

HOT WATER STREAMED DOWN MILES' sore body. He kept touching his cheeks and fighting a blush. Miles had been shameless. He had never taken what he wanted like that. The things he had said, horrifying. He had to go back out there and face Poe again. Fuck. Miles had been a complete glutton for Poe's dick. He had jumped on that massive cock like the thirstiest of whores. Miles didn't regret a thing. He wanted to go again. Instead, he got clean. Miles needed to feed his bear. Wow. His bear. That was exactly what Poe was. He belonged to Miles. Miles would fight anyone who tried to take him. He thought about all the men his ex-husband had slept with behind Miles' back. That had been nothing. Miles would gut anyone who thought to touch Poe. His emotions made no sense. He had never been like this. Miles couldn't help it. It was primal.

Miles mused over his feelings as he dried his skin and found a clean pair of pajamas. He couldn't wait to do nothing but snuggle with Poe. Maybe it was this whole mate thing that had him being all stabby-jealous and cuddly at the same time. Miles supposed he had the rest of his life to figure it out. Hundreds of years, according to Caspian.

Miles headed back to the living room. The couch was empty. Miles' heart tried to drop to his feet.

"*Where are you?*" His mental question sounded panicked. It was out of Miles' control.

"*Kitchen.*"

Relief poured over Miles. He needed to get his feelings in check. Miles padded into the kitchen. He found Poe at the stove, braced on one crutch, and making hot cocoa with all three dogs waiting patiently for anything that might hit the ground. Poe tossed each dog a marshmallow. They took turns jumping to catch them like Poe had trained them in the few minutes Miles had been gone.

"They'll be sugar rushing all day."

Poe flashed him an unrepentant smile. "They're good dogs."

That was true. They deserved treats. Miles moved closer. "Do you need any help?"

"Nah." He seemed to think it over. "Well, I doubt I can carry our mugs to the couch."

Miles joined him at the stove. "I've got it."

Poe looked crestfallen. "I wanted to do this for you."

Miles licked his lips. He was nervous, but he dove in anyhow. "According to Caspian, we have hundreds of years together, so you'll get your turn, I'm sure."

Poe didn't respond.

Miles chanced a glance his way.

Poe's expression was full of so much hope, it stole Miles' breath. "Really? Are you saying you're really willing to be with me?"

Confusion had Miles' eyebrows creeping closer together. "Yeah. I mean, I thought the whole sex thing sort of made that clear."

Poe blushed. His smile made everything right with the world. "Oh. Okay. Good."

He was adorable. Miles had no regrets. "We should take our drinks to the living room and cuddle in front of the fire, don't you think?"

With a nod, Poe snagged his other crutch that rested nearby and hopped toward the living room. Miles followed, carrying their mugs. They settled on the couch and Poe tucked Miles beneath his arm. Several times he kissed Miles' temple, as if he couldn't stop. Miles knew they should trade life stories. He recognized they were still strangers, and they needed to get to know each other. Oddly, none of that felt important. He was at peace with this huge change in his life. They had time. Neither of them were going anywhere. He wanted to bask in the peace of the moment.

"I'll make you proud," Poe said against his temple.

A smile tugged at the corners of Miles' mouth. He knew that. Miles didn't have a single doubt. Something in his heart felt right that had always felt slightly lost. This was the life he had been searching for and never finding. They would be fine.

Chapter Twenty-Five

CHRISTMAS DAY. *One year later...*

ON THEIR FIRST CHRISTMAS TOGETHER, or Yuletide, as Miles had learned Poe celebrated, Poe had whittled Miles a set of adorable bears for the mantel. This year, Miles had given him three more. These were tiny cubs, representing their three dogs. The bear family looked happy together. Miles couldn't stop staring at them.

Poe came through the door, bringing a cold blast of air with him. All three dogs followed in his wake, barking and play fighting all the way to the couch. They greeted Miles before disappearing into the kitchen. Poe dumped a stack of firewood next to the fireplace and peeled off his coat. Miles enjoyed the show.

"I saw Ben while I was out chopping wood." He pulled a white envelope from his pocket. "He gave me another letter from Sean." Poe tossed it in the fireplace.

Miles sipped his coffee to hide his smile. The magic barrier around the town held true. No one with bad intentions could find this place. That hadn't stopped Sean from having letters delivered to Poe in care of the local post office. Their neighbor, Ben, worked there and always sent the letters Poe's way. The first one, they had been scared to open, fearing a new curse. Caspian had cast a binding spell on the letter and then a protection spell on the post office, ensuring no harm came their way. They had read the first letter together. It had been filled with begging and gaslighting, blaming Poe for Sean's cheating while simultaneously pleading for him to come back. Poe hadn't opened a single letter since.

"It's been over a year," Miles reminded him. "Maybe this one said something different."

Poe toed off his boots before crossing the room. He plopped down next to Miles and stole his coffee. After pressing a kiss to Miles' lips, he sipped the drink before responding. "Who gives a shit if it did? What could he say that would matter? I have you: the love of my life. We have our dogs and coffee." His gaze slid down Miles' body. "I have you," he said again.

"You said that twice." Miles tried and failed to keep the humor from his voice.

Poe set the cup aside and tackled Miles to the couch. "I have you." He kissed Miles' lips. "I have you." He kissed him again. "I have you. I have you. I have you."

Miles laughed at Poe's antics.

Poe settled in beside him, keeping Miles squished against his chest. His lips kept brushing Miles' cheek and temple. "I have you," he whispered, making Miles' eyes fall closed.

Poe's hand snaked beneath Miles' shirt. "I love you and only you. No one else matters."

Miles' heart tried doing a cartwheel. "I love you and only you too." It was true. He had never been so in love. It consumed him. Maybe one of these days, he would stop feeling so breathless in Poe's arms, but Miles doubted it. Life was perfect. Yuletide was his favorite time of year now. This was when he had met his mate. The love of his life. His new life had begun in the snow and cold, with a fire crackling in the fireplace. There was no other man or bear out there for him. He thanked every God listening for this life. Miles would make them proud. Poe was the world's greatest gift. Miles would cherish him forever and Poe was right. Nothing or no one else mattered.

Please consider leaving a review at the retailer where you purchased this book. Reviews really help with a book's visibility, which allows me to continue writing more stories. Thank you, Charity.

About the Author

Charity Parkerson is an award-winning and multi-published author with several companies. Born with no filter from her brain to her mouth, she decided to take this odd quirk and insert it in her characters.

*Eight-time Readers' Favorite Award Winner

*2015 Passionate Plume Award Finalist

*2013 Reviewers' Choice Award Winner

*2012 ARRA Finalist for Favorite Paranormal Romance

*Five-time winner of The Mistress of the Darkpath

Connect with her online:

*Sign up for her newsletter: https://sendfox.com/charityparkerson

*Join her readers' group on Facebook: http://bit.ly/CharitysTribe

*Website: https://www.charityparkerson.com

*A list of her social media accounts and giveaways all in one place: http://hy.page/charityparkerson